Iron Promises

A Tale Of Alterra, The World That Is

BY

C.S. MARKS

Iron Promises

A Tale Of Alterra, The World That Is

Cover Art by Hope Hoover
Cover Design by Nancy Roberts
Interior Design by Carie Nixon

Published by Parthian Press, all rights reserved

ParthianPress.com
ISBN: 978-0-9912351-4-8

The Author's Website: CSMarks.com

Chapter 1

Kino, Lord of the Grey-mountain Clan, sat heavily in the great oaken chair in his private chamber, his downcast eyes reflecting the bitterness in his heart. He fingered the long strands of his snowy beard, the coarse waves caressing his hand as would an old friend, or a loving parent. *But my son is dead…*

Kino had many sons, but Noli had been first in his heart. Wonderful, stubborn Noli. Kino had seen himself clearly in his eldest son, the one destined to rule after him. So clearly, in fact, that it was almost embarrassing sometimes. *He was just like me when I was his age…just as pig-headed and strong-willed.* But now the strength was leaving Kino. He had no daughters; that might have been too much to hope for. He had other sons, but he had rarely paid attention to them. He had known all along that Noli would be the one. He had known it from the first sight of him. Now that hope was gone.

He drew a deep, shuddering sigh, trying not to weep again, concentrating instead on his magnificent beard. Was it growing thin? The Dwarves of Rûmm did not tear their beards like those of the Deep-caverns…not since the grief wrought by the War of Betrayal had turned to hate. Kino had not witnessed that terrible conflict, as it had happened long before he was born, but his ancestors had. They had kept the hatred alive, telling the tale through the generations, passed from father to son. Like his father, Kino had learned to hate Elves…but now the hatred was *real*. It had been brought home. Kino would never tear his beard because of an Elf.

His cousin Nimo had brought back Noli's body, cloven by an Elven blade, and told him the tale. Some She-elf had murdered him, no doubt creeping up on him in the dark. *He would have been far too formidable in a real fight. They are cowards, every one of them!* He had looked into the stony grey face of his eldest son, turning aside the soft velvet covering to reveal the terrible wounds beneath.

Now, in his chamber, Kino's old, gnarled hands began to tremble. An Elf named Gaelen had done this. If he ever found her, he would find a way to throttle the life from her.

Belko, Lord of the Blood-stone Clan, was also fingering his beard, but for a different reason. He cursed softly under his breath. Things were not going well between his folk and the Grey-mountain dwarves, and they had gotten worse since the death of Noli, Kino's heir.

Belko shook his head. He and Kino had never been friends, as they were descended from very different lines. His ancestors had committed a terrible crime in the eyes of Kino's clan. *They befriended Elves, and even remained friendly with them after the destruction of Rûmm. The fact that the great Elven-realm of Eádros was also destroyed doesn't deserve consideration, apparently.*

Belko often wondered what had really happened during that dark time. He had rarely encountered Elves, though a few of his people had, usually when traversing the northern Greatwood forest. They used to enjoy trading with some of the river-folk who lived along the Ambros, but that had stopped when the Great Plague had spread to the northern realms. Rumor held that the river-folk were beginning to come back and re-settle in the area, but Belko had learned to live without the goods they provided.

The stories his people brought back had not spoken well of the Elves, who obviously resented the dwarves' intrusion into "their" domain. Their hunter-scouts sent warning shots very near the dwarves' heads, frightening them. As if the forest wasn't frightening enough!

Belko had nothing against the Elves, as his own interactions with them had been hospitable enough. The King of the Greatwood treated his guests with respect, at least. Not so with Kino.

That stubborn old wolverine! What am I going to do with him?

His fingers left his dark auburn beard, now streaked with grey, and clasped an enormous ruby that hung from a massive gold chain around his neck. The Blood-stone—his clan was named for it. And they had found others, too, though none as magnificent as this one. His great-grandsire had discovered it long ago. Belko's realm was rich with the beautiful red gems…at least it had been. Now even the best ores yielded very little, and his people had despaired until they found the new lode—an impressive deposit of ores veined through with blood-stones, blue-water gems, and even the rarest of all—the green emeralds beloved of the Elves. Unfortunately, Kino loved them, too.

Kino's wife, Collena, had the brightest green eyes Belko had ever seen. Now she was gone, but rumor held that Kino believed her spirit lived on in the deep green gems, and he desired them above all others. When he had learned that Belko's sire, Beldar, had traded one of his fine emeralds to the Elves, Kino's wrath had kindled. Relations had been strained ever since.

Now Belko's people had found a new and impressive source of fine gems, to their great relief, but Kino had declared that the ore-deposits—the richest ever found under the Northern Mountains—lay within the boundaries of *his* realm, and that only his people should have access to them. The boundaries between the Clans were not well-defined. In fact, the lines had been drawn in very different places, depending on whose map you were looking at.

Belko knew that at least a small part of the ore lay on Kino's side of the line, but *his* people had found it, they had laid claim to it, and the bulk of it was definitely in the Blood-stone realm. Yes, definitely.

If he thinks he can intimidate me into giving up what is rightfully ours, he will need to think again. My people discovered the Lode, they took the risk, and I won't stand for Kino's trying to usurp it in a fit of temper. I don't care if he thinks part of it is his—he wants it all. He said so. Well, he can take that sentiment and stick it in a very dark place. If he doesn't want to do that himself, I'll be glad to assist him.

In truth, Belko was afraid. Kino's clan was much larger than his own…Fior had chosen to bless them with more females. If the Blood-stone clan didn't bring forth at least a few daughters, and soon, Kino would easily overwhelm them—it would be easy enough already. Belko let out a long, pent-up breath. *Perhaps I should just give him what he wants…*

But Belko was an iron-blooded dwarf descended from the Deep-caverns. His folk were mighty under the Great Mountains. He had to stand up for them here in the north for the sake of his ancestors. *Kino thinks he is stubborn, but he doesn't know what stubborn is. I'll never let him have the Lode…I'll die first. And I'll make sure my sons know it, too.*

Father Mountain, Mother Stone, may I feast well today, thought Croghi as he inched forward on the nearly impenetrable skin of his scaly grey belly. The dwarves were busy mining, their hammers and pickaxes busily delving through layers of rock. Croghi blinked and smiled a little. They would never hear him coming. Eight companions crept along in single file behind him…it had taken awhile to find a way in that was not so accursedly narrow, but they had done it. And now they would have whatever they desired.

Croghi had come a long way from his home lands, the poisonous ruin of Tal-elathas. In fact, one of his own ancestors had crushed the life from many of the Elves of that realm. Croghi already knew he liked the taste of Elf-flesh. He actually preferred it to Dwarf, but one could not afford to be so choosy, and dwarves were juicy enough, though the meat tasted a little like pipe-smoke in his opinion. His massive teeth would make short work of muscle, organs, sinew, even bone. It was his companions, though, that were thinking only of feasting. Croghi knew there were much more appealing and valuable things to be gained from ransacking dwarf-realms. He peered carefully into the cavernous chamber where the little creatures were, as usual, digging things.

He felt one of his companions bumping against his legs, as though urging him forward. He responded by lashing out with his right foot, to the surprise and painful dismay of the one behind him. *We'll move when it's right, and not before.*

Croghi lay unmoving, invisible against the grey stone wall of the chamber, just behind the opening. When one of the dwarves strolled inside unaware, a massive hand snatched him from out of nowhere and crushed his chest, killing him before he could make a sound. *First blood today...*

Croghi would stay hidden until the time was right. Then he and the others would emerge one by one and launch into the unsuspecting dwarves before they could react or mount any kind of defense. He sighed, almost wistful at the thought. Not quite like the old days, but almost as good. He lay as still as living stone, waiting for the right moment. Soon his hands would glow with pretty golden things again.

C.S. Marks

Chapter 2

All men desire to know where they came from—from whom they are descended. Yet Rogond, Ranger descended of the northern realm of Tuathas, had lived nearly all of his life knowing almost nothing of his own origins. Until recently, when he had finally learned the name of his mother, he had thought never to learn anything more. But then he was told of her other son—the brother he had never met. His mother was dead, and he did not know the name of his father, but he had an elder brother whose fate was unknown to him. He clung to this knowledge with the desperate hope of a man who wants to know his family more than anything. And now, he was about to undertake a great journey.

He had sent his friend and fellow Ranger, Thorndil, to the northlands in search of information, for it seemed a fair assumption that, should Rogond's brother have survived the Great Plague, those few Rangers who still roamed the northern wilderness would know most of him. If Thorndil inquired of as many as could be found, he might gain enlightenment. He would then send word to the Greatwood, so that Rogond could follow whatever trail was revealed. As it turned out, it was a good plan.

Thorndil had sent a message back to Rogond just after midsummer's eve, instructing him to travel northward that they could meet on the first new moon of autumn. He had apparently gained some insight into the whereabouts of Rogond's brother from at least one of the Rangers during his travels, and arranged to meet Rogond near the gentle river Eros, the wide stream flowing into the Ambros south of the Northern Mountains.

He was sitting near one of the many flowing springs beneath the tall trees of the Greatwood forest, mulling over the upcoming preparations for the journey ahead, when his beloved Gaelen appeared with a vessel of cold spring water in her hand. She knelt beside him, the wind ruffling her shaggy, dark chestnut hair, blowing the essence of sage and warm summer rain from across the smooth, tawny skin of her shoulders.

Ah,how I love the scent of Wood-elves, he thought, stretching his long legs and flexing his powerful shoulders as she settled into the crook of his left arm. She handed him the vessel of water, turning bright, olive-green eyes up to meet his own calm grey ones.

"I thought you might like a cool drink," she said. "Are you thinking about making ready to leave the Greatwood?"

"Of course I am…I think of little else these days. I only hope my brother is still alive…I pray that I will find him well. That will be a very glad day for me."

"I look forward to that day, too," said Gaelen, idly fingering the long strands of Rogond's dark hair, separating the tangles. Rogond smiled. Gaelen often had difficulty keeping still.

"Who all is going with me?" he whispered. "You are, of course…"

"You won't leave Nelwyn or Galador behind, that's certain," said Gaelen. "And Fima will be going; he doesn't think we can safely draw near to the Northern Mountains without him."

"The Northern Mountains are full of enemies," said Rogond. "A bleak and cheerless place. But there are dwarves there, as well. Fima is right—we will need him if we are to venture there."

"I thought we were going to the Eros…that it was merely a meeting-place," said Gaelen with a slight shiver. No Elf of the Greatwood enjoyed the cold and damp of the northern lands, where even the trees seemed devoid of warmth or welcome.

"So it is," said Rogond. "But I suspect we will have some business nearby…why else would Thorndil have chosen such a meeting-place? The dwarves of the deep-caverns told me that my brother was a Ranger, and that he lived in the northlands. I suspect I will need to go there to find him."

"It can't be that simple, can it?" said Gaelen, her shoulders tensing. "I sense there will be a long and difficult journey, and that your brother will be most difficult to find. Nothing has ever been easy for either of us."

Rogond knew she had a bad feeling about the Northern Mountains, and no wonder—she had been forbidden ever to venture into the dwarf-realms there. "Don't worry," he said, stroking the soft skin of her upper arm with callused fingers. "Hopefully it won't be as difficult as you are expecting."

"I'm sure it won't," she muttered. "It will be worse."

The Company left in the pre-dawn darkness. They would begin on foot, leading their mounts, heading north toward their appointed meeting-place. With them they took stores of food and armaments, for they would need both in such a bleak and cheerless place, where there were many enemies. At least the weather would aid them, for the late summer was fair enough even in the northland. They would need to make their way back south before the onset of winter, however, and even in late autumn the Northern Mountains were sometimes beset by fierce gales that could chill the life from man, Elf, or beast.

The horses—Siva, Eros, Réalta, and Gryffa—stood ready, along with an amiable black fellow named Malvorn. He seemed quite content to bear their stores of food, clothing and weapons, and would prove a worthy companion.

Galador, Rogond's closest friend, a High-elf formerly of Eádros, waited patiently with his life-mate, Nelwyn, who was Gaelen's cousin. Galador—tall, dark-haired, and generally humorless—contrasted with the bright, vivacious Nelwyn, whose golden hair and leaf-green eyes shone with the bright light of a joyful heart.

Rogond and Gaelen checked their gear once again, the last of many such checks, as their dwarvish friend, Lore-master Fima, yawned and stretched his short, sturdy limbs. He was not accustomed to early-morning activities, as he was prone to stay awake far into the dark hours in study and contemplation.

Rogond and Gaelen had not rested, for they had been involved in last-minute preparations for the journey. There was always something that seemed to have been left undone. Now, with the hour at hand, they were reasonably sure of their readiness.

The five companions then departed into the mist—Rogond at the fore with Fima beside him, then Nelwyn and Galador, and finally Gaelen.

They crossed from the King's courtyard through the hidden gates, turning along the bank of the Forest River, following its course. Gaelen and Nelwyn guided them well, knowing that once they reached the river Eros they would have to rely on Rogond and Fima, for the Wood-elves did not venture into the northern lands… not if they could help it. Still, Gaelen sang, as was her habit at the start of a journey. Hopefully, her cheerful song would set the tone for the adventure ahead.

Chapter 3

The Company passed through the north of the Greatwood without incident, though Gaelen's light-hearted departure song had not lasted, as she had been taken with an unshakable melancholy. She regretted leaving the Greatwood, where all was familiar, and she dreaded the hardships that she knew would come. Finding Rogond's brother would be taxing enough, but that was far from the greatest trial she would face. It was her task—her *obsession*—to hunt and kill the creature known as Gorgon Elfhunter.

A task I have failed to accomplish, she thought. Gorgon still lived… she could feel it.

He will show himself again when his strength returns. Until he does, I must aid Rogond. I would not find Gorgon now even if I tried…he is hiding himself from me. She ground her teeth in frustration.

Rogond, who walked beside her, apparently sensed her melancholy mood. He spoke softly, his words meant for her ears alone. "Don't worry, my love. You will see the Greatwood again. I know it."

Gaelen turned her eyes to his as she walked. "And you, Thaylon? Will *you* see the Greatwood again?"

Rogond seemed uncertain, as Gaelen knew he was not given to visions or premonitions. Still, he was insightful enough to realize the magnitude of the tasks before him. He shook his head, looking away from her earnest face toward the path ahead. "I don't know. My future is ever hidden from me. The only thing I *am* certain of is that I will remain at your side to the limit of my fate." Then he smiled. "I have never envied the Elves their foresights, for I may live my life in hope of contentment without fear of contradiction."

Gaelen, who was not fond of such foresights either, stood in agreement, a vague smile on her face. As always, Rogond's forthrightness had aided her in putting things into perspective. She had never placed much faith in the mystical visions of others. She held more faith in her perceived ability to control her own destiny.

The Company reached the borders of the forest, which lay about fifty leagues from the Elven-hold, after nearly two weeks' travel. They had given themselves plenty of time, and no setbacks occurred. This led to much tale-telling and a leisurely pace, which suited Gaelen and Nelwyn, who would linger in the Greatwood awhile. They all tried to suppress the sense of foreboding as they neared the open lands to the north, for everyone knew the peril of them. It was said that dragons lived there, along with Ulcas and trolls, supposedly in great numbers.

Gaelen remembered the hostility of the Northern Mountain dwarves that she had met while in the Deep-cavern realm. *Small wonder their good humor is so thin*, she thought, *with so many enemies to contend with. Still, Elves didn't bring those enemies upon them, and I will never truly understand the nature of grudges lasting thousands of years. Galador's folk lost everything because of the war with the dwarves of Rûmm, yet Galador doesn't seem bent on warring with their descendants. Obviously, Elves are more forgiving and less vengeful.* If Gaelen had known some of the Elven-folk of old, she might have thought differently.

One starlit evening they sat before the fire, waiting for the telling of tales to begin, as Fima rose to his feet and declared that he would favor them with a most riveting account. Nelwyn and Rogond leaned closer to the fire, as Gaelen and Galador turned one ear from the watch. Fima was an outstanding storyteller, and when he was truly on his game his performance was not to be missed.

The dwarf drew himself up to his full height as he stood before them, the red firelight flickering in his deep, dark eyes. He put on a stern expression. "Tonight's tale is not for the faint-hearted. It concerns Fesok the Iron-beard, and his encounter with the great fire-drake that now sleeps in the depths of Cós-domhain. Listen only if you dare," he said. The Elves were now riveted, as tales of dragons were generally quite exciting and frightening. Only Galador had ever beheld one.

Fima threw back his cloak, revealing the glint of the mail-shirt he wore, which was made of steel rings and would turn all but the most determined blade. Over this he wore a simple jerkin of leather embellished with the emblems of the great Dwarvish Houses. He had changed since leaving Mountain-home, where his days were filled mostly with the study of lore, into a hardy traveler who had seen battle in the Barrens against the forces of the mighty Gorgon Elfhunter. Fima's voice and manner were kind, but his eyes and his heart were fierce. He had become very dear to all in the Company. Clearing his throat and blowing a long breath through his snowy beard, he began:

"Fesok, one of the most ancient and revered of all Dwarf-lords, began the building of the great realm of Cós-domhain long ago. Because he was among the first of the Children of Fior, he lived a very, very long life. He is revered by all dwarves, especially those of Cós-domhain, and all of their rulers since were directly descended of him. Lord Grundin, the ruler of Cós-domhain who had received the Company and declared Gaelen Dwarf-friend, is of that mighty line. My present tale concerns one of his most famous exploits.

"Long ago, when the Dwarves were made in the image of Fior, Fesok the Iron-beard found himself deep under the Great Mountains, in that place that would later become known as Cós-domhain, the Deep-cavern-realm. He arose, and began his Great Work, which was to bring together many of the Dwarves of Alterra that they might make the mightiest of all Dwarf realms. All was wondrous in that great realm, and Fesok's folk troubled themselves little with the affairs of Elves or of men, though they fought valiantly when needed. But as Wrothgar's power grew and the Elves were beleaguered, there appeared in the world above many great foes, including Ulcas, trolls, Bödvari, and dragons, the greatest servants of the Enemy."

Gaelen had come to sit by the fire, and she edged a bit closer to it at the mention of Bödvari, for they had been more fearsome than any creature in Alterra save Lord Wrothgar himself. They had brought untold suffering to the Elves throughout their long history. Stories of them would chill the blood of any Elf, and were rarely told around Elven-fires.

"My tale tonight concerns only the Great Worms," said Fima. "Of these, the most formidable are the winged dragons, but they are rare and have not been seen for an Age. The fire-drakes, that breathe flame, and the cold-drakes, which do not, are equally fierce, but cannot fly. Of the ancient fire-drakes, the fiercest of all was quite possibly the great scarlet Worm named Redruin, who was called Ainrath in your tongue. This Great Spawn of Evil did not become known to my people until the middle of the First Reckoning, but when it did, it was fortunate that Fesok himself was there to deal with it.

"Fire-drakes, as with all Great Worms, are known for their ability to confound and beguile any who listen to their tale. Redruin was no exception; all that hearkened to him soon fell under the spell of his words, and were lost. Such was the fate of Elves and men, though it is much more difficult to beguile the Children of Fior. Redruin had wreaked much havoc through the early years of his life, and as he amassed the spoils of his victories he desired a place to keep his ever-growing hoard.

"He had roamed throughout the land in search of such places, but found none to his liking until he found the Great Mountains. Having brought much of his treasure with him, he began his foul exploration of the depths under the mountains, and that is how he came to Fesok's Realm.

"When the folk of Fesok first beheld Redruin, they were amazed at his frightful appearance. He was enormous—no doubt the largest fire-drake ever seen. No other could have withstood him when he was at his full growth, all brilliant scarlet and gold, and heavily armored with fearsome scales. All but the most valiant would quail before the fire of his breath, for it would melt iron and steel. His teeth were like swords, his claws like enormous curved daggers, and his tail bore spines tipped in venom, such that the mere touch of one of them brought instant death."

Here Fima paused, allowing the description to sink in to his audience, his expression deadly serious. Rogond, amused at this gruesome portrayal, knew of Fima's tendency to embellish. The venom-tipped tail spines had not been featured in his prior descriptions of Redruin. Galador, who by this time had come in from the watch, looked rather skeptical, but Gaelen and Nelwyn were much younger and more naïve concerning the nature of dragons, and their eyes were wide, to Fima's delight. Here was his willing audience.

"Ah, yes," he continued, "This was a frightful foe! And he had discovered the Realm of Fesok, where the greatest of all treasure-hoards could be found. Such a prize was irresistible, for all dragons lust after treasure and will do nearly anything to get it.

"Redruin made a plan in his black heart. He knew the dwarves would never suffer him to remain, and they were many and fierce. Even this loathsome creature had heard the tales of the great Dwarf-warriors of the vast Cavern-realm, and he knew they would defeat him and spoil his plan. Therefore, he resolved to take Fesok the Iron-beard alive, and parley with him. He knew that the presence of a dragon in his realm would draw Fesok to him, and when the great Dwarf-lord came to see this fearsome sight for himself, Redruin would take him deep into the darkness, and bargain with him.

"This he accomplished, though the dwarves fought with valor, and many were slain. The Worm took Fesok and lifted him up, pinning his arms so he could no longer wield his great axe, and bore him deep into the darkness. Then he blocked the passage so that the valiant Dwarves could not follow, but would need to go round for miles to rescue their lord.

"When Redruin was satisfied that he was alone with Fesok, he released him, but he had blocked all escape. Redruin had grown to tremendous size and his power was at its height, yet Fesok stood unafraid even as the dragon tried to beguile him with silken words spoken with a treacherous tongue.

"'Hail, Fesok the Iron-beard, Lord of Cós-domhain! I am honored to be in your presence, and beg leave only to parley with you, that we may strike a bargain. Will you hear what I have to say?'

"Fesok considered, knowing that he had no choice in the matter, for he needed to buy time so that he might distract the dragon and recover his axe, which was clutched in the talons of Redruin's right forefoot. Thus he agreed to listen, knowing that dragon-talk may never be trusted, and that he had to guard his mind and heart lest he fall under the spell of Redruin's words.

"'I'm sure you have noticed that certain of your folk have been disappearing of late,' said the dragon. 'I have been feasting on them for a while now, as they are reasonable provender and make good sport, though I must admit that I much prefer the flesh of Elves, as they are far more tender!'

"At this, the heart of Fesok grew hot, for he would brook no dragon feasting on his folk, but he waited patiently as Redruin continued: 'Only recently have I been made aware of the true greatness of your realm, and the vastness of your wealth. We dragons are but humble creatures who desire only modest wealth...but we do crave it. You are a reasonable Dwarf-lord, and I am an honest creature desiring only to add a small amount to my insignificant hoard. Dwarf-treasure is the finest in all the lands, made by the most cunning hands and most perceptive eyes. I would prove to be a capable guardian of your lands. Should we strike this bargain, I assure you that no Dwarf-bane will assail you whilst I live. Do you doubt my power?' He flexed his claws threateningly and blew a small burst of flame from both nostrils.

"Fesok took a step back, for he did not wish to appear to be unimpressed. 'Indeed not, Most Formidable Enemy,' he replied, 'I do not for one moment doubt that you possess great power. But I do not understand why one such as yourself would need to strike such a bargain with us, when you could no doubt take all that we have on a whim. Is that not the case?'

"'Of course it is!' replied Redruin, even though he knew it was not so. 'Yet it's foolish to kill the source of such beautiful and valuable treasures. I would sooner strike this bargain with you— let me remain here, guarding my insignificant hoard and your own lands from all who would threaten them, and in return I ask only a small tribute to be paid twice yearly. I would also beg leave to choose my own items from your no doubt enormous treasury. I can promise that this tribute will be small indeed compared with the valuable service you will receive. I would be your friend, worthy lord, but mark me well—you would not wish to know the fate that awaits your folk should you refuse. What say you?'"

Fima paused dramatically and shook his head. "For a moment, it seemed as though Fesok would be beguiled. He had heard of fearsome servants of Wrothgar that would assail his folk. Would it not be to his advantage to have such a guardian? He stood quietly as though considering the proposal, then asked a question of the dragon:

"'What surety do I have that you will keep your word? And what of my folk? You will cease feasting on them?' At this, Redruin looked wounded.

"'You would not think I would deceive you, O Great Lord, when I could so easily kill you at this moment? Why would I have kept you from harm, if my intention was to deceive? I would have come on you in the dark, and devoured you, and so dealt with one of your descendants, who are not as perceptive or cunning as yourself. I could then easily have beguiled them. All have heard of your cleverness, O Mighty Iron-beard.'"

Fima's voice now assumed a conspiratorial tone. "Of course, Fesok was not deceived, though he nodded in agreement, staring into the dragon's burning, yellow eyes, pretending in that moment that he had fallen under the spell. He had guessed the plan— Redruin would persuade the dwarves to open their treasury, and then he would slay as many as he could manage and claim the hoard for himself. He would be very difficult to rout from that place, and in the process many lives would be lost. Fesok knew that he could trust nothing that came from the foul mouth of the beast, and that he needed to summon his courage and attempt to eliminate Redruin from his realm forever. The dragon was deceived, even as he meant to delude his enemy. He had underestimated the fortitude of Fesok the Iron-beard!"

Galador and Rogond were now making eye contact, and this was a mistake, for Galador was suddenly taken with a snort of laughter that he quickly disguised as a bout of coughing.

"Are you quite all right, Galador? May I continue?" asked Fima with mock concern. He knew the outburst for what it was.

"Quite all right, thank you my friend," said Galador. "Please continue, by all means. I cannot *wait* to hear the exciting climax."

"Fine. Where was I? Oh, yes…Fesok knew that he could not trust the dragon's words, yet he feigned falling under the dragon-spell so that he might catch Redruin off guard.

"'O Most Fearsome and Terrible Disaster, I find your offer quite generous and irrefutable. Yet we must seal the bargain. Let us do so at once, that I may be free of this confinement, for though I risk offending you, being in such close quarters with your formidable breath has taxed me. So, let us complete our bargain: I, Fesok, do promise to pay tribute twice yearly to the Great Worm Redruin, on pain of death, and to allow him to select his own tribute from my treasure-stores. In return, said Worm will cease his feasting on my folk, and will guard my realm from all who would threaten it. Is that right?'

"'Quite correct, O Most Reasonable and Discerning Dwarf-lord, whose decision is indeed wise,' said the Worm. 'Do we have an agreement?'

"'We still must bind our bargain with a symbolic gesture of trust. Extend your right forelimb, and I will clasp it, and we shall be in agreement,' said Fesok. The dragon considered, for the untrustworthy are ever unwilling to trust. Yet he looked into the vacant eyes of Fesok, thinking he was beguiled, and cautiously extended his forelimb. In doing so, he left Fesok's great axe upon the ground.

"As Fesok walked blankly toward him, reaching out to clasp a mighty claw in his right hand, he suddenly sprang forward and seized the axe. 'Foul worm of Wrothgar! No bargain will be struck this day! Your doom is at hand!'" Fima's yell was so loud and ferocious that even Galador jumped.

The old lore-master proceeded to describe a great battle between Redruin and Fesok, in which Fesok performed supernatural and heroic feats of skill and daring. This was punctuated by gestures, beastly roars, and fierce battle-yells as Fima leaped about, totally engrossed in the telling. Finally, the heroic Fesok vanquished the dragon, though he was nearly incinerated and was wounded in the process by one of the venomous tail spines.

"But, Fima," said Nelwyn, "I thought you said that to be pierced by those spines meant sudden and instant death!"

"Did I? Oh…of course I did. But I was then referring to ordinary folk, not the greatest of all the ancient Dwarf-lords. Fesok was sickened by the venom, but he did not die, for he was made of the hardiest material. Besides, he was learned in dragon-lore, and knew that the antidote for the venom was the blood of the dragon."

"But, Fima," Gaelen chimed in, "I thought dragon's blood was deadly poison! I learned that when I was very young. Is that not so?"

"Of course it is, to *ordinary* folk, as I said before," said Fima, realizing that he was losing control of the moment. "Will you please allow me to continue? My tale is nearly finished."

"Sorry..." said the Elves in unison.

"At any rate, Fesok, who was in *no way ordinary*, managed to heal himself using the blood of the dragon. The two poisons thus counteracted each other. Yes, that's it," he said, casting an eye at Gaelen and Nelwyn. "And the Worm was defeated."

He paused, as though his tale was now complete, but Gaelen spoke again. "How awful! He was blocked in with a stinking dragon-carcass, with no food or water, and his folk could not reach him! However did he escape?"

"Hmmmm...yesss," said Fima, stroking his white beard. "I shall continue. Ahhh...it seems Fesok was blocked in with no food or water, and his folk would take many days to free him, though they worked day and night. When they finally broke through, they found Fesok lying as though in the sleep of death, and they were grief-stricken. But then, just as all hope had left them, Fesok roused himself and opened his eyes, lifting up his head, and spoke to them as they stood astonished before him: 'Yea, even now I have awakened, for...for the great Lord Fior came to me, and granted to me a great sleep, that I might be saved from death!'"

Fima looked around at the Elves, wondering whether they had accepted this unlikely explanation. Galador rose to his feet, and began to applaud.

"Well saved, my friend, well saved!"

Gaelen, Nelwyn and Rogond, all clapped in earnest, for they all loved Fima and his tale had delighted them. Fima suspected they didn't believe a word of it, but his scowling soon gave way to laughter. In this he was joined by his friends, as the moon rose high and the tale-telling continued beneath the field of brilliant stars.

Early the following afternoon, the Company stood at last with the trees at their backs, gazing out over the wide, rolling land that led into the foothills of the Northern Mountains. Here the ground was rocky, but there was still plenty of grass for the horses, who took immediate advantage of it. "Don't fear, Eros. The grazing will be fine for a while yet. It isn't necessary to take every blade of grass with you," said Rogond, who was having some difficulty lifting Eros' head to lead him. Eros seemed unconvinced, his jaws working as he moved methodically across the grassy ground, cropping all in his wake.

"Let's linger here, and let them eat their fill. They've been making do for a while," said Galador, who was having similar difficulty with Réalta. So the Company waited near the edge of the forest, where the last of the blackberries were swelling in large numbers. Gaelen and Nelwyn had soon picked several pints each. Here in the North the autumn would come earlier, but for now they all enjoyed the unmistakable taste of summer. The dark, sweet juices filled their mouths, staining their lips and fingertips.

Fima lay back in the mid-day sun, his belly filled nearly to bursting. "Ahhh! That was a fine, fine repast. I would suggest that we try to take some of those along, for it may be awhile before we see such bounty again."

Gaelen and Nelwyn had shared this thought, for they had already gathered enough extra berries to feast upon for days, and were lamenting the fact that they probably would not have time to dry some for later in the journey. Though blackberries lost much of their flavor during the drying, and were full of seeds, the Elves knew they could not turn up their noses at such provender. They didn't know how long their stores would last, or when they would be replenished.

They decided to remain in the shadow of the forest until dawn, for traveling in darkness would be far more dangerous as they drew closer to the mountains. The new moon was a little more than a week away, and that would be plenty of time to travel the distance to their meeting-place. Even so, they set a good pace. They would travel now only in daylight, and the Elves would all keep watch during the dark hours as Rogond and Fima rested. The horses made excellent sentinels as well, for they would react to any whiff of Ulca, troll, or other evil creature. The Company risked no fires, drawing their cloaks about them for warmth, and they told no tales after nightfall.

Gaelen caught the scent of trolls just after moonrise, four days after leaving the forest behind. The horses became restive, confirming her fears.

"How many trolls, do you think?" asked Nelwyn.

"I think…I think there are three," said Gaelen, testing the breeze with her sensitive nose. She climbed down among the rocks to where Rogond and Fima lay resting, sheltered from the wind. She roused them and told them of her discovery, for all would need to be alert should the trolls approach.

"Nelwyn and I wish to investigate. The Company will be in peril should a group of trolls decide to attack in darkness. I would determine their numbers and their intention. If need be, we will divert them from this place." Gaelen looked over at Fima, whose weathered face was full of doubt. "Do not fear, Lore-master. We're accomplished in this sort of thing. We have been leading enemies astray for a thousand years." She waved her hand dismissively, as though putting herself in the path of a group of trolls was nothing to be concerned about.

"No doubt you have," said Rogond, who knew differently. "But always in your own lands. Are you certain this is necessary?"

"Trolls do not venture into the Greatwood, Rogond. They need to be able to sleep below ground when the sun is up, and the forest is mostly bereft of suitable hiding-places. Nelwyn and I have encountered them in places other than our own lands. Have no fear!"

Her bright eyes and eager voice told Rogond that she looked forward to this challenge, and he knew better than to dissuade her. He also knew she was right—the Company could not risk an encounter with a group of trolls. He nodded, to Fima's astonishment. "Be swift, and learn only what you need. Do only what you must do. This is not a game."

Gaelen's eyes glittered, and she quirked a smile at him. It gladdened his heart, for he had not seen her truly smile since leaving the Elven-hold. "Not a game? Of *course* it is!" She shook

21

her hair from her eyes with a toss of her head, grabbed her bow, and disappeared into the dark.

After she had gone, Rogond moved to stand beside Galador, who was looking to the northwest, and placed a hand on his shoulder. "You surprise me, my friend. It has not been in your nature of late to allow Nelwyn to go with Gaelen into potential peril."

Galador sighed. "You are my closest friend save Nelwyn, Rogond, and yet there is much about me that you don't know. The choice wasn't made lightly, and I'm not happy about it. Yet I know that Nelwyn must do as she wills, and that I must not interfere. She is skilled and sensible. And as much as I hate to admit it, they are right. We must know our enemy. I only trust they will not act beyond their skill in diverting the trolls."

Rogond, who would have liked to say "Don't worry…they won't," remained silent.

They stood for some time with neither sight nor sound of the Wood-elves nor of any enemy. Then they heard sounds that froze their blood—fearsome roars, the thunder of huge, heavy feet, and the crash of stone—echoing from the north, moving eastward. No one moved or spoke until dawn broke, as Eros and Siva nickered softly toward the east, from whence Nelwyn and Gaelen made their appearance at last.

Nelwyn embraced Galador, who noted with some dismay that she was shaken and a bit pale. Her cloak was torn, and her hair in disarray. She would not speak of the night's events, and Gaelen would only state that the trolls would give no trouble.

Though disheveled, she appeared quite bright and cheerful as she greeted Rogond and Fima. Her eyes burned with a fierce light, and she seemed in quite a good humor as she sat honing the blade of her curved short-sword after first wiping the thick, black troll-blood from it. She began to sing under her breath as Rogond knelt beside her. He looked up into the disapproving face of Galador, who shook his head slightly, then mouthed the word *Fire-heart* with a wry expression. Rogond had to admit, as he sat listening to Gaelen's rather lusty battle-chant, the comparison seemed almost apt.

The Company reached their destination three days later, having crossed the river, which in late summer was shallow and presented no difficulty. The new moon would take place in two nights, so they watched and waited for signs of Thorndil and his companions. They made camp on the banks of the clear, pleasant Gilien stream that flowed from beneath the very rock of the mountains before joining the river Eros.

Gaelen didn't like the look of those looming mountains, and even Fima seemed uneasy, for it was said that this land was under sway of evil, except in the dwarf-holdings. These were neither large nor extensive, and the dwarves were beset by many enemies.

Fima told of the coming of dwarves to the Northern Mountains. "Many were descended from the folk of Rûmm, but there were a few also that had come from the Deep-caverns, seeking to carve out their own realms. I say with some pride that they created some of the most beautiful things ever seen—their craftsmen forged weapons that would rival any made by the Elves. In fact, my ancestors often worked in partnership with the Èolar and were quite friendly with them." Fima, who was descended from the Deep-caverns, had retained his ancestors' open-minded attitude toward the Elves, thus finding welcome in Mountain-home as Chief Lore-master to Lady Ordath.

"But now it is small wonder that the dwarves of the North have lost some of their good humor," he said. "They are beleaguered, and these lands are not as rich in precious metals and gems as those beneath the Great Mountains. Yet some would say it is better to have a realm of one's own, though it be less mighty. Such is the mind of these folk; should we encounter them, it would be wise to remember."

Fima described the perils of the Northern Mountains, as the Company sat in solemn silence. Though they had only encountered the three hill-trolls, they had seen some evidence of Ulcas as well. They remained wary and kept their voices low, awaiting the arrival of Thorndil and his companions. Finally, in the darkness of the new moon, Gaelen reported the Rangers approaching, for she had caught their scent on the wind.

Soon Thorndil appeared, along with two other hardy men of approximately the same age. They approached the encampment with caution. Thorndil turned to his two companions and spoke briefly with them before calling out: "Hail, Rogond and Company. If you are here, which we know you are, please show yourselves to your friends. We are no Ulcas!"

Rogond rose from concealment, greeting his friends with enthusiasm. When the rest of the Company emerged, Thorndil introduced his companions—Dergin, who threw back his hood to reveal flaming red hair, and Turanor, who stood nearly as tall as Rogond.

After satisfying hunger and thirst, the Rangers settled down to rest for the remainder of the dark hours. They didn't blame Rogond and the Company for being wary of them, and, though they had passed through these dangerous lands without incident, they knew they dared not linger long.

Turanor drew Rogond aside. "Thorndil has told me what he knows of your history. You are the second son of Rosalin, as I understand it, and now you wish to learn all that you may of her firstborn, your brother. Is that right?"

Rogond looked earnestly into the eyes of Turanor, for he had seldom wished for anything so much. "Yes. I hope you will enlighten me, and yet not bring ill news. I pray that my brother still lives, and that I may find him, for I have not known the name of my mother until recent days. My brother may not even know of my birth, for I was not even a year of age when my mother's family was killed. What enlightenment can you give?"

"Who named you 'Rogond?' Is that the name given you at your birth?"

Rogond shook his head. "I do not know my given name. Rogond is the name the Elves gave to me, for they found me inside a cleft of stone. Why do you ask?"

Turanor drew his cloak against the rising wind. "It will storm before morning, I fear, and rain tomorrow." He looked up at the black sky, in which the stars could no longer be seen. The lightning was already flickering in the west—these storms swept down from beyond the Monadh-ainnas, the dreaded Fire-mountains. Of these, no descendant of Tuathas would speak, for their wrath had doomed fair Tuathas to ruin.

Rogond sat as patiently as he could, waiting for Turanor to continue. He had known Thorndil for years, and if Turanor was anything like him, Rogond knew he would speak only when he was ready. Turanor drew forth his long clay pipe, filled it slowly and deliberately, and set it alight, blowing sweet, blue smoke from his lips with an expression of contentment on his weathered face. Several minutes had passed in this manner when Gaelen appeared suddenly from behind them, startling Turanor such that he nearly dropped the pipe from his hand. He let out a deep breath, favoring Rogond with a wry expression.

"Will you not answer his question?" Gaelen asked Turanor in a slightly impatient tone. "Why do you delay? Can you not tell that Rogond is anxious? He has waited long and traveled halfway 'round Alterra for enlightenment...all the way to Cós-domhain. Can you not smoke and talk at the same time?"

Turanor smiled. "A friend of yours, Rogond? You seem to be keeping better company than when last we met."

Rogond flushed, touching Gaelen's shoulder gently to calm her. "She is a very good friend, but I fear she has little patience sometimes."

Turanor chuckled. "Then I had better speak now, for I have no desire to incur her wrath. She would no doubt startle me to death the next time."

At this, Fima, who sat nearby keeping one ear on the proceedings, chimed in. "I've been wanting to hang a bell on her for a long time, but my friend Rogond has prevented me."

Gaelen smiled wryly. "That's not the only thing preventing you! It's not my fault your ears can't detect me over the racket of your own breathing. But let's hear Turanor's tale, since he now seems ready to tell it."

Turanor took one more long drag on his beloved pipe before putting it aside. "First, Rogond, let me tell you that I do not know whether your brother still lives. Neither do I know for certain that he does not, so that's the good news. So many of our folk perished during the Plague, but both your brother and I were far away beneath the Eastern Hills when the sickness came." He glanced over at Gaelen. "To answer your question, I asked about the source of your name because the first son of Rosalin was named Hallagond."

"Rogond, his name is much like yours!" said Gaelen.

"A coincidence," said Rogond, turning to Turanor. "I don't know what name my mother gave me."

Turanor nodded. "It's an interesting coincidence that your names are so similar. In other respects you are much alike in appearance, with the same grey eyes and dark hair. Hallagond bore a scar across the back of his right hand from an Ulca-blade. His voice was not as deep, but was…rougher, somehow. You were raised by Elves, and it is evident in your manner of speech, whereas Hallagond grew up in Dûn Bennas, among men."

"Hallagond," said Rogond, savoring the sound of his brother's name, so like his own. "It means 'tall-stone.'"

"Yes, though he was not as tall as you are," said Turanor with a smile. "Yet he might have been even taller had his height matched his attitude. When he matured he came to the northlands seeking adventure, and he traveled with us, gaining renown as a skilled fighter. He showed great perception and intelligence, and we came to look up to him, for he was a natural leader.

Along with myself and several other comrades, he took to wandering the region where we are now sitting, convinced that the Dark Powers were trying to establish a new stronghold here. Hallagond seemed to have an affinity for dwarves, and he befriended them, often coming to their aid. Then the rumor of the Plague reached us.

Hallagond wanted to return to Dûn Bennas to aid his family, but knew such an effort would prove futile. By the time we became aware of it in the North, the Plague had already swept through that great city, killing nearly everyone in it, including the King. It was said that the fires that burned the bodies of the dead sent up smoke that could be seen all the way from heaven."

Turanor paused for a moment, his gaze distant, his eyes pained. Lightning flashed in the western sky, and the thunder grew louder as the storm drew nearer. Shaken from his private thoughts, he continued.

"The dwarves convinced us to retreat to the Eastern Hills, and to shelter belowground so that we might survive, for the pestilence had spread northward like an evil, stinking wind, killing untold numbers of men in its wake."

He looked over at Rogond. "I would expect your mother, Rosalin, left Dûn Bennas in a vain effort to escape it. It's a good thing you were found and fostered by the Elves, who were no doubt traveling to Tal-ailean. If your mother had not been set upon by Ulcas, and you had remained with her, there is little doubt that you would have died. The sickness would have found her and her folk; their deaths at the hands of the Ulcas may have been the easier to bear. It was not a good death, the Plague…from my understanding."

Here he paused again, his brows drawing together above haunted eyes. He had lost friends and family in that dreaded scourge—few living men were untouched by it. "At any rate," he continued, puffing once more upon his pipe, "the Rangers who fled to the Eastern Hills survived, for the Plague spread to the north and west. But the people of the southlands suffered great loss. Many families perished down to the last man. Hallagond and I longed to give aid to them, but we knew that to travel there would mean near-certain death, and it was necessary that at least a few of us remain to carry on the line. The Blood of the Tuathar survives…barely."

Gaelen and Nelwyn shivered in the darkness at the thought of a scourge that would take man, woman, and child without mercy. They would not be able to imagine such a horror, as they had never been subjected to the indignity of illness and never would be. "Was it…like when we first found you?" said Gaelen, turning to Rogond. "You were stricken suffering a fever that nearly killed you…I know I won't soon forget it."

"It was worse…much worse," said Rogond. He looked over at Turanor. "I had a bad chill and a fever when Gaelen found me. I will always remember her song…it saved my life."

"It made you fall in love with her, is what it did," muttered Galador, who had overheard. Rogond flushed crimson as Turanor, wide-eyed, raised both eyebrows before turning grim again. "This was no mere fever," he said. "People died in two days, raving and bleeding and spewing foulness…it was horrible. But the aftermath might have been worse. People turned on one another, often blaming the survivors and claiming that they were responsible for bringing the sickness among them. They burned many people alive, I'm told…especially in the sutherlands."

Gaelen grew quite pale at the thought, as Turanor shook his head. "At any rate, after two years had passed since the last rumors of the pestilence reached us, we decided to venture west again to see what could be salvaged. It was a grim journey. We looked to the dead as we could, burning the untended bodies, despairing as we found so few of our folk alive. Evil things had come into the northlands then, for our people were no longer able to keep them at bay, and we couldn't stop their creeping into those empty lands, working their evil. It was a dark time."

"Hallagond was still with you then, yes?" asked Rogond.

"He was, but then we separated. He and a group of Rangers supposedly went eastward, but none returned. I later learned that all save Hallagond had vanished, and I was somewhat surprised to hear that he had then fled back to the Eastern Hills. I have neither seen nor heard anything of him since. That was, let me see…perhaps five and forty years ago?"

Turanor drew a long draught on his pipe, as though lost in thought. "We didn't understand why he left us, but we have neither seen nor heard from him since. The Eastern Hills are largely uninhabited, though dwarves have spoken of delving there. What business would Hallagond have there? We do not know. As I have said, we don't even know for certain that he still lives. He was a dedicated Ranger…what other course would have kept him from his duties? We all wonder what became of his companions."

Turanor looked into the eyes of Rogond, his expression grave. "Some have guessed that your brother has either gone mad, or has somehow lost his honor."

Rogond took in a sharp breath. To a Ranger, the loss of honor was a fate much worse than death. "You've guessed, but you don't know. There are many explanations possible. You have said that you don't even know where he is, or whether he has fallen. Why would you stain his name with such a speculation?"

"Hallagond would neither abandon his people, nor fail to bring word of the fate of his companions, unless too ashamed to do so. I knew him as well as anyone, and called him friend. He would only retreat into solitude if he could no longer suffer our company, and there is only one reasonable explanation for that. He was a supremely honorable man, Rogond. Such a man expects perfection of himself, and when he falls short of that goal it's sometimes difficult to live with the consequences. But you're right—we do not know the particulars of his fate. It's possible that he encountered an evil so fearsome and terrible that it deranged him, but I think that unlikely."

Turanor paused, as though considering. "If you would learn more of Hallagond, you should go first to the dwarves of the Northern Mountains, for they knew much of him. It's my hope that he renewed his ties with them on his way to the Eastern Hills, and he may have made his intentions known to them. I have not inquired of them, as I found them somewhat difficult to deal with, but since you have brought a dwarvish guide with you, all may be well. Look for a dwarf named Belko; he is the head of the clan that sheltered us here. Hopefully he still lives. If not, his eldest son is called Beori."

"I know of this Belko. He is said to be a reasonable fellow," said Fima.

"That he is, though he is a hard enemy," said Turanor. "He'll want something in return for his aid, for dwarves give away little without recompense. I wish you good fortune in finding him, and in bargaining with him. I'm sorry that my tale does not gladden your heart."

Rogond nodded. "That it does not, my good Turanor, for I would almost rather have learned of my brother's death than of your speculation. All the same, I'm forever in your debt. You undertook a long journey to bring this news, and I thank you. I must now continue my search, find my brother, and learn the truth. Perhaps he can be healed, and his honor restored, if indeed he thinks it lost. Will you go with us into the mountain?"

He felt Gaelen tense at those words. No Elf enjoys the thought of going into underground dwarf-realms, especially not those shared with so many enemies. And Rogond knew that wasn't the only problem. Due to an unfortunate incident in the Deep-caverns, Gaelen was forbidden to venture into the Northern Mountain-realm, on pain of death.

Turanor shook his head again. "No, my friend, I cannot tarry here, as my duty calls me elsewhere, though I will show you the way.

We can also take your horses to a place of safety, for they cannot venture under the mountains."

"You won't need to show us the way," said Fima. "I traveled these paths long ago. I know where to find Belko and his clan."

"Fima, is this Belko a relative of Nimo, or of Noli?" asked Gaelen.

To her relief, he shook his head. "I don't believe so. If I'm right, Belko's folk are descended from the Deep-caverns. They were armorers of some renown, if memory serves. We may even be distant kin. Do not fear." He turned back to Turanor, and explained. "We were involved in a rather unfortunate conflict last year, Gaelen in particular. We may encounter difficulty should we meet with certain of the folk here, for none of us will be welcome, not even myself. I hope our tale has not spread to *all* the dwarves beneath these mountains."

Rogond turned to Turanor. "Perhaps Fima and I should go alone, and leave the Elves under your watchful protection. After all, this is my errand, and I would rather not risk their lives in this pursuit. Certain of the Northern Mountain dwarves would hold great enmity toward them." He glanced over at Gaelen, who appeared astonished that he would even suggest such a thing.

"They would, in fact, kill Gaelen on sight," said Fima, as if to remind her.

After a moment's pause, she spoke in a calm, level tone that made clear no such argument would be heard by any of the Elves. "Though I cannot speak for anyone but myself, I expect we will all go under the mountain together, or none will go at all." To emphasize her pronouncement, she drew one of her long daggers and cast it without error into the nearby limb of a dead tree, where it quivered convincingly. "We are ready, Aridan. I will be taken not easily by any enemy under the mountain. After all, if I cannot hide from dwarves, I might as well just give up in disgrace."

Both Turanor and Rogond nodded assent, their eyebrows lifted as they met her fierce, bright gaze. She drew her cloak about her as the wind rose with the advent of the rain. She retrieved her blade before returning to the watch, sitting alone upon her rocky vantage point, visible through the grey rain only when illuminated by the occasional flash of lightning. Rogond smiled to himself. It looked as though the Company would be going beneath the mountains tomorrow…all of them.

Chapter 4

When the dawn came the storm had passed, but the rain had settled in for a long stay. The Company shivered as they shouldered their provisions and prepared to go into the dark passages beneath the mountains, leaving the horses in the care of Turanor and Dergin. They would be taken to a safe place and well cared for; the Company would return for them when they had learned what they could from the dwarves of the Northern Mountains.

"This realm was known in our tongue as Harnian, the Iron-realm," said Fima. "Its people are called Rûm-harnen. Three clans dwell here, two of Rûmm and one of Cós-domhain…the clan of which Belko is descended. A good thing, as Galador would not be welcomed into the loving arms of the descendants of Rûmm. They will never forget the loss of their great smiths and craftsmen at the hands of the Elves."

"And so will the descendants of Eádros not forget the loss of their King, their beautiful city, and their way of life," replied Galador grimly. "Our memories are long, and there are even those yet living among my people who witnessed the fall of the City of Light. I share no love for the dwarves of Rûmm."

Thorndil and Rogond walked beside Fima and Galador, shaking their heads. "You must put such thoughts aside, for we may yet encounter these folk, though we seek the clan of Belko," said Rogond. "Galador, you must swallow your pride and suffer them, or we are lost. If you cannot, then perhaps it would be better for you to remain with Turanor."

"Peace, Rogond," said Galador. "I am not a child. I know when to suppress my pride, and I understand the importance of my silence before the dwarves of Rûmm. Besides, do you think I would leave you in the company of Gaelen, who somehow manages to annoy folk even without speaking to them?" Gaelen, who walked behind him, rewarded his comment by picking up a large pebble and tossing it down the back of his tunic.

Fima turned and smiled over his shoulder at her. "We could do worse than walk in the company of a Dwarf-friend of Grundin, and our worthy Rogond is also Dwarf-friend. With luck, Galador, *you* will be the largest of our worries." Galador turned and inclined his head to Gaelen, though his smile was somewhat strained as he wriggled his right shoulder, trying to shift the pebble from beneath his tunic. She smiled back at him, for she knew the pebble would remain until he removed his sword belt and allowed it to fall free.

Turanor had aided Fima in choosing the way that was most likely to lead them to Belko, and they continued as quietly as they might down the dimly-lit passages. The air in this place was wholesome enough, but still seemed stuffy and somewhat stale to the Elves, who preferred the fresh breezes aboveground.

As they drew deeper into the mountain, the passageways became shorter and wider, such that many of the Company would soon have to stoop to avoid bumping their heads on the ceiling. They had plenty of torches, but lamps and torches had been placed along the walls, giving enough light to travel by. These seemed to be increasing in number, and Fima, who walked ahead, cautioned everyone to be wary, for he believed they would soon encounter the Rûm-harnen.

"There may be traps when we are this close, so be cautious and tread lightly," he said. "And touch no stone, nor any gold or precious artifact that you may see. My folk are known for setting terrible traps for thieves." No one doubted this; they all knew of the legendary wrath of dwarves against those who would steal their possessions.

Gaelen smiled at being told to "tread lightly" by Fima. She could hear his footfalls and his breathing over everyone else in the Company put together. Still, she took his meaning. It was the Elves, not Fima, who would arouse the suspicion and ire of the dwarves. She was very glad to be in his company.

Soon the passage narrowed such that all had to drop back into single file. Fima explained that this was a device designed to protect the dwarves, as large enemies would have quite a bit of difficulty negotiating the way in, and could be easily picked off one by one.

Soon it was quite difficult for any save himself and Gaelen, who was smaller than the others, though she was still considerably taller than Fima. Thorndil, in particular, was having trouble. He was in some pain from having to travel stooped over, for he was getting older and had suffered many wounds over his lifetime.

Rogond knew that his friend was distressed, and he called a halt. None save Fima could fit comfortably in such tight quarters, and the Elves in particular were dismayed at the cold stone walls that seemed to close in around them. Rogond was mindful of Thorndil's pride as he addressed the Company. "This path is difficult for us, and it seems to me that we might be better served by sending Fima ahead to scout the way. The rest should retreat to the wider passage and wait for word that we will be welcomed. What say you, Fima? Do you agree?"

Fima nodded, though he did not relish traveling the passage alone. "I know that you tall folk are at odds in this realm," he said. "I, on the other hand, am quite at ease. I shall be happy to scout the way and make our presence known to Belko's clan. I should encounter them before long, and I expect no trouble."

Gaelen and Rogond knew Fima well, and they could tell from his voice and his manner that at least some of this confidence was false. If he did have trouble, he might well find himself in serious difficulty alone.

"I will go with Fima, for he may need a companion," said Gaelen, who was relatively small and flexible, and could walk the narrow way with less hardship than the others. "No one should walk this way alone. I know that I will be safe in the company of such a guide."

Rogond cast a worried look at Galador. As the tallest among them, it made no sense for him to attempt the passage, but he did not like the thought of Gaelen walking into peril without him, though she was right to suggest that Fima not go alone. "Will she be safe with Belko's people, Fima?"

"I can't say, but they are my kin, and I know they have long feuded with the other clans here...those descended of Rûmm. Our people were friendly with Elves, you see, and that makes us lesser dwarves in some folks' opinions."

After one last hesitation, Rogond nodded toward Gaelen. Her eyes were bright in the dim light; she was clever and capable, and would guard Fima faithfully. She bowed her head in acknowledgment, handing him her longbow, as it would hinder her in tight quarters.

As Fima and Gaelen started down the passage, and the others turned about, Nelwyn paused. She and Gaelen had always gone forth together, facing tasks with determination and fortitude, knowing each stood in defense of the other. After speaking briefly to Galador, she pushed past him and followed Gaelen out of sight.

The passage had narrowed to the point that a dwarf could still walk comfortably, and could still swing an axe with relative ease. Fima walked ahead of the two Elves, who were forced to travel with bent backs and bowed heads. As they drew farther and farther from their companions, Fima began to lag back as though he sensed something amiss. He stopped moving forward, and Gaelen looked at him quizzically. "What's wrong?" she asked in the dwarf-tongue.

Fima smiled and replied so that Nelwyn would understand. "I don't know, but I have an uneasy feeling that will not leave me. I cannot help but wonder why we haven't encountered any of Belko's folk, for this was a well-used passage upon a time, and I have neither seen nor heard any sign. Yet, there are lamps and torches, so someone has been along this passage fairly recently. Can you read anything by the scent?"

Gaelen closed her eyes and sampled the air from the passage ahead, concentrating hard. Fima watched her with fascination as her brow furrowed, then relaxed, then furrowed. She took a step forward, taking in a few additional short, sharp breaths. Finally, she opened her eyes. "I smell dwarf, and…perhaps troll? I am catching a vague scent of troll. The dwarf is someone other than yourself, begging your pardon. I detect three separate scents in addition to your own…and the troll-stench is very faint."

Fima looked at her in wonderment. It was the dwarves' custom to travel in threes, which Gaelen probably did not know. Truly, her ability to track by scent was amazing. He had learned of other Elves who had developed similar ability, all of them legendary trackers, for such prowess was rare even among Elves.

"Perhaps the troll-stench is that which remains on our clothing after our encounter with the three we slew the other night," suggested Nelwyn. "I can still catch a whiff of it every now and then." She wrinkled her nose slightly, for troll-stench was so unpleasant that she could not imagine even other trolls tolerating it.

"True enough," said Gaelen, "but this is different, as it comes from the airway of the passage, and not from you or from me. And it's fresher...the scent on you is beginning to wane."

"Not soon enough for me," muttered Nelwyn. "*Arrah!* You had to suggest that diversion, didn't you? Oh, it will work, Nelwyn... don't worry, Nelwyn...I'll be right there, Nelwyn. Indeed!"

"Well, it *did* work. I *was* there...eventually. And you needn't have worried had you done it right...was it my fault you slipped on that stone and gave yourself away before I was ready?"

Gaelen neglected to mention that she, too, had slipped on the rain-slick stones, and had nearly come to a very bad end. Both Elves had been very lucky that dark night. It was just as well that no one else in the Company would hear the details of it.

"Peace, both of you," said Fima, who was beginning to worry. "How recently did the dwarves pass this way? Can you determine that?" At this, both Gaelen and Nelwyn bent to examine the signs visible to the eye, working their way up the passage to learn what it would tell. Fima followed them at a respectful distance, for he had no tracking skills and did not wish to distract them.

It took the Elves some time to detect anything, as the stone of the floor was well worn and polished, and would hold little sign. At last they learned what they needed to know. "I believe the tracks are recent, no more than a day old," said Nelwyn. "And there were three, as Gaelen has indicated. But the same sets of tracks turned about, and made their way back."

"Hmmm...that makes very little sense to me," said Fima. "But there is nothing of fresh blood or death in the air, or you would have mentioned it. Let's go on, but cautiously. We should be nearly to Belko's guard-chamber."

They started down the passage again, and soon they did indeed come into a deserted guard-chamber. There were some disturbing signs, and they knew the cause before they entered the chamber. Gaelen commented that not only had the troll-stench grown stronger, but that she now caught the scent of old, dried blood. Here was the evidence of disaster: the walls and roof of the guard-chamber has been broken apart, apparently by something very large and strong. The chamber was in complete disarray, with useless, broken weapons scattered about, and more evidence of battle. Here was the dried blood, mostly dwarf-blood but some of the thick, black stuff of trolls as well. There were many tracks, very easily seen now, as they were bloody. Gaelen looked at them and whistled under her breath.

"If that is a troll-print, it's the largest I have yet seen," she said.

Fima's face was grim. "We must go back. We will gain no entry into Belko's Realm by this road. The passageways have been blocked." He was right—all ways leading from the chamber were now impassable; solid barricades of rock stood in their way.

"Who blocked them?" asked Nelwyn. "How did trolls get into this place, when the passages leading in are so narrow?"

"Not all of them are narrow," said Fima. "The main passage from the guard-chamber led into the Great Hall, and it was wide and tall. A troll would have needed to enter from that way, but could easily have done so. That is a most unsettling thought." He indicated a huge pile of stone that now blocked that passage.

"But surely your folk are more than capable of dealing with a troll," said Gaelen, who had just slain three of them with only the aid of her cousin Nelwyn. "After all, trolls dwell under mountains, so dwarves must encounter them often. Yet this scene looks as though the dwarves were bested. How could that be?"

"I don't know," said Fima, "but I fear for them. This chamber has seen disaster recently, and Belko's folk may have taken grave damage. I hope that is not the case."

"Well, at least three of them were alive in the recent past," Nelwyn encouraged. "Is there any other way that we might take, so that we might learn the truth?"

"Yes, but we will need to go back out of the mountain to find it," said Fima, "and it will take us near to the realm of Noli's folk. I was hoping to avoid that." He shook his head, his lined face looking ancient and weary in the torchlight. He picked up a broken axe from the ground. "Somehow, I sense that this troll was not of the ordinary sort, but we will need to venture into peril to learn of it."

"Well, there is much that must be learned, Fima, and we are not learning it here. Lead on," said Gaelen. "I'm not afraid. Perhaps it is not as you fear, and the dwarves, though they may have lost comrades, are well enough. It does not change the fact that we must find Belko for Rogond's sake. I would learn what I may as quickly as I can, for the sooner I emerge from this dark way, the happier I'll be. Lead on."

Gaelen's point was well taken, but her friends knew that some of her bravado was false, for she drew both of her bright daggers, and her lithe frame was tense as she followed Fima back down the way they had come.

The Company emerged from the mountain several hours later, following Fima's lead. Now there would be another decision to make, for the original plan could not be followed. "We must take another path into the mountain," said Fima, "and it will lead us near to the descendants of Rûmm, the kin of Nimo and Noli. Noli was the son of Kino, who rules that clan."

All in the Company knew that they had been warned never to venture into Nimo's domain. He had unjustly blamed Gaelen for the death of his cousin Noli in Cós-domhain. Enough time had surely passed that the northern dwarves would know of Noli's death, so it was perilous for Gaelen, Galador, or Nelwyn to venture there. Even Fima was unwelcome in the realm of Noli's kin, for he served the Elves of Mountain-home. No Elf or Elf-friend would find welcome among the descendants of Rûmm.

They stood under an overhang of rock, sheltering from the rain, as Fima and Rogond put forth a proposal. They would go into the mountain together, leaving the remainder of the Company, for Rogond was the only one among them seeking knowledge of Hallagond, and Fima alone knew the way. Thorndil immediately protested.

"The dwarves don't know my name or my face," he said, "for I did not go with you into the Realm of Grundin."

"I will not be left behind," said Galador. "The way will be difficult, and you may face hardships other than unfriendly dwarves. My bond of friendship is stronger than my fear. Gaelen and Nelwyn should probably remain outside the mountain, but I would go beneath it."

"And why should Nelwyn be left outside?" asked Nelwyn. I went not into Cós-domhain, and I am not of Eádros! If anyone here will arouse the ire of the dwarves of Rûmm, it's you and Gaelen." Here she turned to her smaller cousin, speaking gently to her. "I'm sorry, but Rogond is right this time. You will be in peril if you go with us."

Gaelen stood calmly, cleaning her nails with the tip of one of her long knives. "You are all going to be in peril under the mountain," she said. "It would be my suggestion that we do our best to avoid the Noli's people in the first place. What would you have me do, mind the horses? Do you honestly believe I could do that while my friends walk into the dark?" She smiled, but her eyes were hard. She shook her head slowly. "I think not."

"You are all missing the point of this proposal," said Fima, shaking his head in frustration. "The Elves are being asked to remain because they will bring peril to those who go below…Gaelen in particular! We will be set upon merely because you are with us, if we encounter the wrong folk. Do you not understand?"

Gaelen raised her eyebrows. "Yes, Lore-master, I understand. But we both know that there are perils in the Harnien that will be far beyond two Aridani and one dwarf, begging your pardon. You will have need of us. If you insist that I remain behind, then I will, but you will have need of my bow and my blades, and they won't be there to aid you. Consider well your request of me."

Fima and Rogond spoke quietly aside. At times they would gesture, raising their voices as though in heated argument, but in the end they approached, the pain in Rogond's face evident as he stood before the Company. Fima cleared his throat and addressed them all, drawing himself up and doing his best to look important. "Do you all promise to abide by Rogond's and my decision?" he asked. The Elves looked at one another.

"We do," said Galador. "What choice has been made?"

"All except Gaelen will go under the Mountain. Nelwyn may choose to remain with her or to go with the Company, but Gaelen must follow Turanor and aid him in looking after the horses. This is an important task, and should not be taken lightly." He looked into Gaelen's bright eyes. "You risk too much under the mountain, little Wood-elf, both to yourself and to us. This is the only right path. Do you understand?"

"For the second time this day, I *do* understand, Fima. But you're making a mistake, though your intentions are well founded. You will know it before you see daylight again."

She turned to Nelwyn. "What say you, cousin? I see in your eyes that you would rather go with Galador. That's most likely a good thing, for the Company will have need of you, particularly Galador of Eádros! He seems to forget that the dwarves of Rûmm hate the Elves of Eádros with the heat of a thousand suns. In fact, I wonder whether Fima has considered that. I will stay behind, since you cannot suffer my company, though I still believe we should all remain together. Choose your path now."

Nelwyn felt as though she was being torn in two. Her cousin stood before her, having been singled out, feeling no doubt shamed and unhappy. Yet the Company walked into a place where foes abounded, and they would have need of her bow. "You will take care of yourself as you always have, Gaelen," she said. "I'm not worried for your safety. I must go with Galador and Rogond, for they may need my aid. It's not my wish to separate, but I do see the sense in Fima's plan. You dare not risk this road." She embraced Gaelen then, and turned to stand with Galador.

Gaelen moved aside, sitting down upon a stone, and calmly regarded the Company. Her eyes fixed on Rogond, who looked levelly back at her, though he obviously found it difficult as he spoke to her. "I will return soon, and then we shall know where our path will lead next. I will have more need of your skill than ever, and I will not ask that you part from us again if I can help it, yet Fima is right, and you know it. He thinks it unlikely that we will be able to avoid Noli's folk. Therefore, though it grieves me, I must agree with him. Now, give me your promise that you will remain here."

Gaelen nodded. "I will remain here."

The Company made ready to depart. Gaelen sat upon a stone, watching them dispassionately, as they once again set out with Fima leading them. All said their farewells, promising to return, and she wished them well. She watched as they disappeared into the rain, Rogond and Nelwyn turning back at the last, raising their right hands to her. She returned the gesture, her face impassive. *I promised to remain. I didn't say for how long...*

She would be true to her word, and would remain in this place for a time, but her road would not lead her to Turanor and the horses. She would follow her beloved Rogond. That was a vow she had made while still in the Greatwood, and she would not break it. The Company would have need of her, and she would be there to aid them, though they would not know it. Gaelen Taldin, the silent-footed, would follow them unseen and unheard, for such was her nature, and she could do nothing to alter it.

Fima directed the Company up a steep and narrow path that led along the mountainside for miles. They picked their way carefully through the unrelenting grey rain, for the wet stone path was slick and treacherous, yet they needed to make haste. The darkness would soon be upon them, and it would do no good to be out in the open.

At last they reached the place Fima was seeking. It appeared to be an ordinary cave in the side of the mountain, but when they entered they discovered a passage blocked by a door of carven stone inlaid with bronze medallions. Fima, ever the lore-master, looked over at Rogond with a twinkle in his eye. "What can you make of this, Aridan?" he asked.

Rogond studied the runes upon the door. "It says that we must speak the names of the Five Founders to enter. This is knowledge that I do not possess. You alone among us know their names."

"Ah! Don't be so hasty—read on," said Fima, chuckling to himself.

Rogond did so, and then he smiled. Dwarvish folk reputedly had little humor in them, but that was not his experience. He reached out toward the door, pressing two of the medallions, and stepped back. The door swung inward slowly, to the delight of Fima.

"Well done, my discerning friend. You have not forgotten your studies, even after years in the wilderness. It should please you to know that this way is not so crowded as the one from whence we came, so you may rightly hold your head high. Walk with me."

The Company then walked through the doorway, Fima and Rogond leading. Fima paused long enough for the door to close behind them, which it did on its own after a minute or two. Galador strode up beside Rogond. "So, how did you know the way to open the door? It seemed to be some kind of joke…will you share it?"

"There are some very small runes beneath the larger ones, written right to left, admonishing that the names of the Five Founders must not be uttered, for only dwarves may know them. Rather, we should press the medallions of 'friend' and 'enemy.' The one indicating a friend had Fior's hammer graven on it, and the other…well, let's just say the image is unflattering, and it most likely applies to you and Nelwyn."

"Hmmph," said Galador. "I can only imagine. What is it? A horse's hindquarters?"

"Something like that," said Rogond. "It would be difficult for non-dwarvish folk to translate the message and thus gain entrance."

"Your people are clever, Fima, I'll give you that," said Galador.

It soon became apparent that the passage was seldom used. "We'll need to avail ourselves of our own torches now, as there are none along the walls," said Rogond.

"I do see the dim blue light of Elvish lanterns," said Nelwyn, "but they are not many, and their light is not adequate to travel by."

"They are used only as markers," said Fima. "Still, that's a good thing—they will aid me in choosing the correct path."

43

The Elves shivered, remembering their experience under the Great Mountains, for these passages strongly reminded them of it. Yet here they had torches aplenty, as well as Fima to guide them, and they were not so dismayed.

All at once, the Company froze in its tracks as they heard the rumor of feet approaching from the passage in front of them.

"Put away your weapons, and be ready, for the folk of the Harnian approach," said Fima. "We'll need our wits and all of our considerable charm to be accepted by them." He looked pointedly at Galador. "Remember, speak only when you must. I will do the talking here."

So saying, he planted his feet and stood in the forefront, facing the dark way ahead, where the first torchlight could now be seen. Soon the dwarves appeared in disturbingly large numbers.

"Just our luck," muttered Fima. "They are descended of Rûmm."

The dwarves did not appear to be in the mood to extend a friendly welcome. As they approached, their faces were fierce, and they gripped their axes tightly. They halted in front of Fima, grumbling among themselves as they beheld the remainder of the Company. Their hostility toward the Elves was palpable.

Fima held out both hands to show that he held no weapon, bowing low before them, addressing them in the dwarf-tongue.

"Hail, most worthy folk of the Harnian. I am Fima, son of Khima, your most humble servant. We seek enlightenment from Belko, Master of one of the three Great Clans of the Rûm-harnan. We mean no intrusion, and meant to come by the lower path, but found the way was blocked. We are concerned, and hope that Belko and his folk have not fallen upon evil times. Can you enlighten us?"

"Why do you seek enlightenment from Belko? What is your true purpose? I cannot imagine that even dull-witted Elves would venture here, where they're not welcome. What sort of enlightenment could possibly interest them?" The speaker, a dark-bearded fellow with bright black eyes, had not returned Fima's courtesy by revealing his name. He now stood with his arms folded in front of him, as his folk muttered in agreement.

Fima regarded him coolly. "Your name, my good dwarf, so that I may address you properly," he said. "Our need for enlightenment

44

shall remain our own for the moment, begging your pardon. And we have done no harm to you or to your folk. We would be forever indebted if you would deign to guide us to Belko, whereupon all will be made known to him and to you, if he wills it."

The dwarves muttered among themselves, as the one who had spoken glowered from under his dark brows. "We will speak no more of it," he said. "You are in no position to bargain, Fima, Loremaster of Mountain-home! You think we do not know your name? You will follow us now, and no argument. We will relieve you of your weapons first—refuse at your peril! When we reach our destination, our folk will hear your tale and decide your fate."

He then spoke to his companions, and the Company was surrounded. "Hand over your weapons, and do it gently," said Fima in a soft voice, still looking calmly at the dark-bearded dwarf. All did as they were told, though reluctantly, and Rogond hoped that none of his friends would come to grief in the pursuit of what Belko could tell.

The dwarves both led them and prodded them from behind as they made their way deep into the heart of the mountain, where Kino, sire of Noli, led the second clan of the Rûm-harnen, founded by the descendants of the lost city of Rûmm.

Gaelen had waited for several hours before following behind the Company. The path Fima had led them on was difficult to locate in the rain, and had tested her tracking skills, for the Company was moving cautiously and had left little sign for her. She came at last to the cave and the hidden doorway, shaking her head in frustration as she translated the difficult inscription. She did not know the names of the Five Founders, yet she could not imagine Fima uttering them before non-dwarvish folk. There had to be another way.

She looked down at the tiny runes below the main inscription, but they made no sense when read from left to right, and she was confounded. She reached out with her right hand to clear some of the dust, and as she brushed the inscription carefully from right to left, the first words became clear. *It's written…backwards.*

45

The runes were reversed, but the words were still in order from left to right, though they were all run together in a continuous stream. That made things even more difficult, but Gaelen was undaunted, sitting patiently before the door until she managed to translate the message, at least in part.

She looked at the bronze medallions, studying the designs. *The hammer of Fior is evident, I should think it would mean "friend," but which would be the sign of an enemy?* Here was one that resembled a troll, but that was surely too obvious. She pressed it anyway, and nothing happened.

Most of the others were simply pleasing ornamental designs, but…what about this one? Why would dwarves, especially those of Rûmm, have a medallion showing what appeared to be… well…a very beautiful jackass? A jackass with a seven-pointed star emblazoned on its rump? *Oh, ha, ha,* thought Gaelen, scowling as she pressed it, together with the other, knowing she was right this time.

The door opened, as it had for the Company earlier. Gaelen stepped through, hoping that the way would be well lighted, for she had surrendered her torch to Fima. "You won't be needing that," he had said, looking at her with slight distrust in his deep blue eyes. She had handed it over without hesitation, not wanting him to guess her plan.

Now she wished she had somehow managed to keep hold of it, as the door closed behind her with a heavy "thud." It was dark here; no torches had been lit, but Elves have very keen sight, and Gaelen's was keener than many. The few lamps placed as markers would serve. Gaelen would follow her nose, and track the Company slowly in the dark, keeping from sight and hearing until they accomplished their purpose and emerged from the mountain. They would never know that she followed them unless they were beset by enemies, and then she would aid them. Fima would be angry with her, and she hoped she would not lose his friendship, but she had to remain true to Rogond, and to herself.

The dwarves of the Harnian led the Company into a beautiful hall of stone, where many of their fellows were already assembled. This was undoubtedly the Hall of Council, where matters were debated and decided. Rogond noted many beautiful things, and evidence of great skill in delving, carving, and craft. Yet this realm was but a shadow of the greatness of Cós-domhain, as Fima had foretold. Still, it was a fine hall, with cascading fountains of pure spring water, carved pillars of stone, and arched ceilings and doorways. There were tapestries hung about the walls, and many lamps and roaring fires made the hall both bright and warm.

Galador, who had lived in one of the fairest underground cities ever built, could see the influence of Rûmm in this place, for Eádros was delved, at least in part, by the dwarves of that lost city. He shook his head—such a tragic end for two such great and beautiful realms.

Many of the dwarves glowered at the Company, but not a few looked upon them in wonderment. Not all dwarves were as thick-headed as the likes of Noli and Nimo. Even so, as the Council sat before them on their raised dais in chairs of carved stone, it became clear that the Company would need all the skill they could muster to find welcome here.

Chief among the clan was an ancient, white-bearded fellow named Kino. Noli had been his eldest son. Fima could tell from his somber attire that he was still in mourning, though his long, white beard was not torn.

Kino drew himself up before the Company, glaring at the Elves in particular. "Declare your names and your intentions, for you are trespassing in the Realm of the Harnian without leave. Fima, you are known to us already, and are not held trustworthy, for you have forsaken your own people to live among Elves. You are distant kin to some of our folk, and thus may escape unharmed, but we must learn of the intent of these strangers. Depending upon what we learn, they may not be as fortunate."

"Peace, Kino of the Harnian," Fima replied. "My Company and I are here to serve. We seek the clan of Belko, for this worthy Aridan would learn of his heritage, and the dwarves of Belko may aid him in his quest. That is our sole purpose in being here. We tried to take the lower path into Belko's domain, but found the way had been blocked. We seek him now both for enlightenment and to make certain of his safety, for it appeared as though his folk had been beset by enemies. Perhaps you know what has befallen?"

"I do," said Kino, "and I will provide enlightenment. But first, you must enlighten me! You must tell of the death of Noli, my worthy son and heir, at the hands of an Elf in Cós-domhain. You will do it alone, for we must imprison those who travel with you. No Elf or Elf-friend will I suffer to walk freely in my realm!"

At this the dwarves moved forward, and set the Company in bonds. Fima urged them to submit quietly. "This is...a little worse than I expected. I am going to need to talk us out of this, and I will need your help," he said, casting a worried look at Rogond.

Fima then addressed the old dwarf: "Wait, most noble Kino, before you take the younger Aridan away. He knows much of Noli's death, and he is true of heart. Please, if you would gain this knowledge, let him stand with me. We will tell all that we can." He turned to Rogond and muttered in the Elven-tongue: "Be glad, my friend, that your face and your eyes are guileless." The Elves and Thorndil were led away, no doubt to be locked alone in dark cells of stone with thick, wooden doors. The dwarves handled them none too gently.

Fima and Rogond stood bound before Kino and the Council, as the dwarves of the Harnian looked on. Fima began the tale of their journey into the Realm of Grundin, again to seek enlightenment for Rogond. He told of Gaelen, and at the mention of her name Kino bristled and his eyes blazed, for it was known to him. Then Rogond told of Gorgon Elfhunter and the evil he had wrought upon the Elves. He told Kino that it was Gorgon, not Gaelen, who had slain Noli.

"Why would a creature that hates only Elves slay my son, Aridan?"

"Gorgon hates all things that live, including himself," Rogond replied. "Yet I believe he slew Noli, and another dwarf named Tibo, so that he could bring suspicion and anger upon our Company, especially Gaelen, who is his sworn enemy. He thought that the dwarves would then drive us forth, or even kill us, but Lord Grundin saw through the plan. Still, we left the cavern-realm, for

Gaelen would not remain there and bring further trials upon the dwarves, though she was grievously hurt. For this, Grundin named her Dwarf-friend."

At this, all the dwarves muttered among themselves. Many did not believe Rogond, for they respected Grundin, and Gaelen had not been thus flattered in Nimo's reporting.

"That's certainly not the way the tale was told to *me*," said Kino, his eyes ablaze. "Where is this Elf, that she may prove herself to be Dwarf-friend? Grundin would have given her some token. Where is she?" He shook his head in disgust. "I don't believe a word of this—no Elf would be made Dwarf-friend by Grundin, surely!"

"We left her behind. She did not come with us into the mountain because we feared your wrath toward her. She is not here," said Fima.

"That was no doubt well-advised, but now seems convenient. Very convenient. How do we know that your entire tale isn't a pack of preposterous lies?" Kino looked hard at Rogond as he spoke, but the Ranger looked straight back at him, his grey eyes calm and earnest. There was no lie in them.

"Well?" asked Kino, who was becoming irritated. "Why do you not speak?"

Rogond shook his head slowly. "What would you have me say? I have spoken the truth of the matter, but you will not hear me. You only hear what Nimo tells you, and Nimo did not witness all that happened. If you cannot see the truth, I cannot convince you, for the truth is all I have to offer."

Other kin of Nimo and Noli then spoke in anger, for they did not care for Rogond's suggestion that their kinsman's accounting of Noli's death might have been less than accurate. "Will you stand there, Kino, and allow this man to claim that Nimo has spoken falsely? Nimo had nothing to gain by it, whereas these strangers have everything to lose! They're obviously up to no good, and now that we have caught them they'll say anything to gain your favor. Why have we not heard of this 'Gorgon Elfhunter?' Why have none of our folk ever heard even the mention of him in tales or songs, if he is such a great scourge?"

"You have not heard of him because the Elves only recently became fully aware of him and of his nature," said Fima. "He has been preying upon them for many long years, but always he has made certain none lived to tell of him. He is a terrible enemy! I would not have believed in his existence until I saw him with my own eyes. And he takes victims of all races. Elves he prefers, but we have known him to kill men, dwarves…even Ulcas. He is alone, and allied with no one."

Kino raised his hand, and all were silent. "First, if this creature enjoys killing Elves, I might want to reward him for it. I am disinclined to believe you, Fima. I will not give credence to a lap-dog of Ordath over our own kin, and I see no reason to trust this Ranger, though he lies well and convincingly. I do not detect treachery in him, but sometimes the most treacherous folk are those who appear honest."

He turned back to Rogond. "Why, then, should I believe you, Aridan?"

"It may interest you to know that Rogond bears a token declaring him to be Dwarf-friend," said Fima, who was not especially upset at being called a "lap dog of Ordath." He had been called far worse before.

"Is this true?" asked Kino. "Why did you not mention it? Show us this token then, if you would prove that Fima is not a worthless liar."

Rogond shook his head. "I do bear such a token," he said, "but I did not mention it because it was given to my mother, and not to me. I only inherited it. I felt that you might believe such status had been given directly to me, or that I was claiming it, and I would not mislead you."

"Well, show us now, then, and be quick about it," said Kino, who honestly did not expect Rogond had any sort of token in his possession. When the Ranger handed him the ring, Kino glared at him with suspicion. Calling for one of the blue lamps, he examined the ring with wonder. His eyes widened as he read the inscription deep in the heart of the black stone: "I, Farin, declare the bearer to be Dwarf-friend, and free in Dwarf Realms."

"Farin is one of the greatest smiths of the Deep-caverns," said Kino, "and he is akin to our folk on his mother's side. Yet Nimo has told us that he proved untrustworthy when Noli was slain, refusing to believe the truth, and he interfered with Nimo's pursuit of vengeance upon the Elf. He even threatened Nimo, from my understanding."

"Actually, Kino, I was there," said Fima. "Farin merely protected me from Nimo, as he and his folk were coming dangerously close to bashing me with their axes. Farin was merely standing up for the rights of the Elf, who had been made Dwarf-friend by Grundin, his lord. Any of your folk would have done the same. Does it not seem strange that Nimo has claimed none of these folk are trustworthy except himself? Perhaps it is Nimo who is deluded...overcome by grief, no doubt. I know you are kin, my good Kino, and so you must believe him until otherwise enlightened, but is it not possible that he is mistaken? He would hear no defense of the Elf, despite the fact that there was no real evidence against her that had not been provided by Gorgon Elfhunter, *who was the real killer of Noli!* Nimo was one of the few who actually believed the lies told by the enemy. In so doing, he ended up being the unwitting servant of Noli's killer! You say you would reward Gorgon...would you really reward the creature who tore the life from your son?"

Several of the dwarves gasped in horror, and Nimo's folk cried out in defense of their kinsman. "So now this Elvish lore-master challenges the worth of Nimo, who sits upon the Council of Elders in Grundin's Realm as the representative of the Harnian! Is he saying that any dwarf so entrusted could possibly be lacking in wisdom?"

"For that matter, I also sat upon that Council, and had done so for many years," said Fima. "I merely point out that perhaps Nimo's grief and prejudice blinded him to the truth. He was very quick to blame the Elf, which doesn't surprise me. He made his enmity toward her plain from the first, though she treated him with courtesy and respect. Believe me, with this Elf in particular, that is saying something."

Kino's face had flushed dark red beneath his white beard. "I regret saying that I would reward anyone who would take the life of my son," he said. "But I need time to consider what I have heard. Aridan, you may have a token naming you Dwarf-friend, but it was not given to you. I am impressed that you did not use it falsely, however, and will take this into my deliberations."

51

Rogond bowed his head respectfully, secretly thankful that no dwarf present had encountered him on the Great Dwarf Road, when he *had* used the ring to secure safe passage for himself and the Elves.

"You will be taken to a cell and confined there until I have considered this matter," said Kino. "You and your friends will be cared for until your fate is decided. I may wish to hear from you again, and if so, I will bring you before me. Enjoy your time in waiting until then."

Rogond and Fima tried not to appear too worried as they were led away to be imprisoned. They were locked in separate cells, but could speak to one another through small grates in the walls between. They were also pleased to hear that Nelwyn, Thorndil and Galador were well, as they had been locked up nearby. Yet they would now have to wait in this place until Kino decided what to do with them, and they were no closer to their goal of finding Belko. Kino had not yet enlightened them as to the nature of the mysterious findings in Belko's guard-chamber, though he claimed to know of it.

Rogond worried about Gaelen. If they were kept here for a long while, would she grow restless and come looking for them? Of course she would. Rogond began to pace restively up and down the small floor of his cell, unaware that Gaelen was already drawing near to the Council-chamber, trying to learn all she could concerning his fate.

Gaelen had pieced together much of what had befallen the Company from the signs left behind. She knew they had been approached and surrounded by dwarves, and that they had been led down the passage. It was now a good thing the way was not well lighted, for she would sometimes hear voices and the loud clamor of feet. Then she would disappear, springing lightly up onto a ledge or shrinking back into a cleft of stone, away from torchlight, until the dwarves passed her by.

She might have been expert at remaining unseen and unheard, but now her luck was running out, for the passage had widened, and the many torches placed along the walls meant that this way was well used. She would not be able to hide here, so she took a dark and narrow side passage, hoping it would eventually lead to her friends. She made many turns in the dark, but her memory for place and path would serve her well. She was soon rewarded, crouching upon the shadowed ledge overlooking the Hall of Council.

Here she observed a rather large group of dwarves engaged in lively debate. She tried to pick up snatches of their meaning, as they were speaking their own tongue, and she blessed Fima and his willingness to instruct her. After a while, she realized that her friends had been imprisoned, and that the dwarves were even now trying to decide their fate. The kin of Nimo insisted that Rogond and Fima not be trusted, were obviously lying, and needed to be locked away forever along with the Elves. It would not disappoint them, in fact, if the Elves were slain at once, in payment for Noli. This "Gorgon Elfhunter" was obvious fiction.

Others argued that Fima had once sat upon the Council of Elders in Grundin's Realm, even as Nimo did now. The Elf who had supposedly killed Noli had been named Dwarf-friend, and they really had no proof of anything one way or the other.

Gaelen's blood grew chilly, then hot with indignation as she listened carefully to this exchange. When it finally ended, the dwarves were no closer to a decision. She drew her cloak around her, taking notice of Kino, whom she rightly guessed to be in charge of the Council. Gaelen wanted to go looking for her friends, and to free them, but she knew that this would never work. She could not remain unseen forever; if caught she would be imprisoned with them and would not be able to come to their aid.

Much that she had heard dismayed her. *Nelwyn and Galador are certainly at risk... the dwarves won't wait long before acting. I have to do something, and soon, for they might kill my friends simply to avoid having to deal with them.*

In truth, Gaelen needn't have worried so, for dwarves are not savages and were unlikely to kill helpless captives, but she had heard otherwise in tales over the years. Fima was extraordinarily civilized, but that was most likely due to his spending so much time in Mountain-home. And though she had found Lord Grundin and his folk to be quite admirable, even likeable, it was clear to her that Nimo and his kin were far more dangerous.

She considered the paths before her, which were few. She needed help to rescue her friends, but what aid could she summon here, in the Harnian? Then a thought struck her, and she mulled it over in her mind for several minutes. It would be difficult, to be sure, and it might not work even if she could accomplish it, but it was the only path open to her, and she would take it. When she was satisfied that she was not running headlong into total disaster, she rose quietly to her feet, picked up her weapons, and made her way back the way she had come.

She took one of the last torches to be found along the passage wall, knowing there would be none for the remainder of her journey to the doorway. She didn't know whether the same command would open the door from the inside, and there might be an inscription that she would need to decipher in order to make her escape. She hoped it would not tax her beyond her limited knowledge of the dwarf-tongue, or that the riddle of the doorway would not be beyond her cleverness. She scented down the passageways, testing the air for signs of activity, listening intently, all her senses trained. *It will be difficult to hide with a torch in my hand...*

She mulled over the words spoken by Noli's kin in the Great Hall. They all believed that she had slain Noli, and some had even suggested killing Nelwyn and Galador in payment for it. She felt her face grow hot again as she thought of it. *Do they not understand that Gorgon intended to bring suspicion upon me? Obviously not, for deep in their hearts they want me to be guilty...it justifies their hatred.*

Gaelen vowed that no dwarf would harm Nelwyn or Galador without suffering grave penalty at her hands. Even as she ran, her blood rose and her grip tightened on her longbow. She very nearly took a wrong turn, for the way out was intricate and she could not afford distraction, so she put such dark thoughts from her mind. Besides, she trusted Fima. He would surely convince Kino if given the chance. After all...he had convinced her that dwarves had virtues, hadn't he? In fact, Fima had become one of her dearest friends. She no longer looked upon his folk in the same way as she had, and never would again. She hoped that Kino would hear Fima's words.

Her plan was to return to the other passage, the one ending in the guard-chamber leading to the Great Hall of Belko's folk. *Someone is maintaining those torches. If I wait long enough they will appear. Then I must convince them to take me to Belko, and try to persuade him to aid my friends…*

She did not yet know how she would do this, but she was Dwarf-friend of Grundin, Lord of the Great-caverns. Fima had said that Belko's folk were akin to those of that realm.

I hope it's enough…

She finally drew nigh the doorway, and brought the torch near such that she could see any inscription upon it. There was none; the door was smooth, polished, and absolutely plain to her eyes. There were no medallions to press. How in the world was she supposed to open it? *Most likely, I'm not supposed to open it*, she thought. No doubt this was a device to keep clever enemies from escaping. *Well, that's exactly what I am to them, isn't it…a clever enemy?* Yet she had to get out of this doorway, for she did not know these mountains and would surely lose her way if denied the chance to follow familiar paths. Frustrated, she examined the door once more lest she had missed something, but found no mark either with sharp eyes or searching fingers. She extinguished the torch, for she did not want to attract anyone to find her trapped in the doorway. Then she sat upon the ground, her knees drawn up before her, considering her choice of paths.

None were very appealing. She might wander in the maze of tunnels beneath the mountain, searching for aid, or she might try to find the place where her friends were imprisoned and attempt to free them, though they were no doubt heavily guarded. Not even Gaelen would be stealthy enough to accomplish that task, and she knew it.

As she mulled over the rather absurd thought of returning to the Great Hall and presenting herself to the dwarves as ransom for her friends, she was shaken back to her senses by the sound of voices coming from outside the doorway. She could hear them through a wide, iron-barred grating made for ventilation—the deep, gravelly voices of dwarves, speaking in their own tongue. Gaelen could not make out what they were saying, but she knew that she had to conceal herself quickly. She backed against the wall behind the stone door, even as it shuddered open, hoping that it would not press all the way back against the wall and crush her.

Three dwarves stood before the ever-widening doorway; apparently they had been tracking Gaelen and her friends to determine who it was that had found their way to the hidden entrance. They shook their heads, muttering to one another. Gaelen shrank back (thankfully, the door had not crushed her), keeping from their torchlight. She would have to be quick, for though the door would close slowly, she would need to spirit herself through it without being seen, and the dwarves were wary. They looked this way and that as they continued their discourse, and Gaelen heard several words that she recognized, including "Elves" and "enemies." She peered around the doorway, still holding the now-dark torch in one hand, trying to determine when they might turn away from her such that she could escape. Then she noticed a brooch worn by one of the dwarves—it was fashioned of hard silver, with the emblem of a helm and hammer overlaid with the seven silver stars of the Èolar.

This was encouraging. Was it possible that these dwarves were in fact the very ones who had been sent to monitor the lower passage, and they had detected signs of the presence of the Company and then tracked them here? If so, Gaelen would bless her luck. If not, she might soon find herself at the mercy of Kino's folk. As the dwarves drew farther from the doorway, the heavy door began to move closed. Now was the time for action one way or another. They had turned from her; she could slip out unnoticed, but then she would miss the chance she sought, and it might not come again.

One of the dwarves uttered the name "Beori," and Gaelen remembered that he was the son of Belko. That, and the fact that Noli's kin might at any moment decide to do harm to Nelwyn, decided her. When the heavy doors closed, blocking the light from the world outside, Gaelen stood before them, facing an uncertain fate as she cast her weapons upon the ground at the feet of the three astonished dwarves, who had been taken completely unaware.

She held her hands out, palms upward, and bowed before them, speaking a greeting that Fima had taught her: "Hail, worthy craftsmen, may your beards grow long and your hands flow with wealth." Then, she looked up into their suspicious, surprised faces, and added in a halting voice, "Ummm...I come in peace?"

They drew their axes from their belts, but kept their weapons lowered as the one in the center took a step forward, his dark eyes wide. "Hail, Elf of unknown realm. How came you to learn the speech of the Rûmhar? You are not of the Harnian—that is plain. Your dialect would indicate you learned from the folk of Grundin. Answer quickly, for we are not inclined to trust you."

Gaelen kept her hands clearly visible as she spoke. She was truly at their mercy, as she held no weapon. She chose her words carefully. "I was taught the Dwarf-tongue by a lore-master of Grundin's realm, and I am Dwarf-friend," she replied. "Yet my mastery of your tongue is limited. If it please you, I would now speak the tongue of the Aridani, for the many intricacies of Rûmhul confound my meager ability." In truth, her speech was far less eloquent, but the dwarves at least appeared to get the gist of it.

They bowed low, though they kept their eyes on her always. The one in the center spoke again. "Fair enough, we shall speak the common-tongue. Yet you have learned more of our speech than any Elf of my acquaintance. You had best be Dwarf-friend, or my axe shall have words with the one who instructed you in it," he growled. "Tell us your name, Elf, and where it is that you hail from."

Gaelen thought for a moment. "I am known as Taldin, and I am of the Greatwood Realm," she replied. "I would now ask the same of you, for I seek the folk of Belko, and pray that you number among them." At this the dwarves turned and muttered in low voices. Then they gave their names as Kari, Feori, and Noro, who had spoken first to Gaelen.

"We know of the fell forest of the Darkmere," said Noro, his grey brows lowered. "It is a terrible place, and the Elves there are not our friends. How came an Elf of that realm to be named Dwarf-friend? You had best have proof of this claim; otherwise we shall take you before Kino of the Clan of Rûmm. He has no love for any of you! His son, Noli, was slain by an Elf, we are told. He will truly appreciate the chance to deal with you, I'm sure!"

"I'm sure you're right," said Gaelen, "but I *am* Dwarf-friend. If you would have the proof, allow me to provide it." She sat down before them on the stony floor, and set about the task of convincing them.

Rogond and Fima had been brought before Kino as he sat in his private audience hall, where he had been conferring with others of his Council. "I trust your needs have been met as you await our decision," he said, "and that your confinement has not discomfited you unduly."

"Not unduly," said Fima, "Though the Elves may disagree. Your people have not treated them with as much courtesy as they might wish for, when they have done nothing to deserve this hard treatment. Still, you have not damaged us, and we must be grateful for that."

"Indeed you should. Perhaps you do not remember the sight of my son hanging dead upon a spike, though you claim to have witnessed it," said Kino, his hands clenching slightly upon the arms of his oaken chair. "I will forever remember his ruined neck, cloven by an Elven blade, as he rests now beneath this very mountain. He was my eldest son, Fima Lore-master, and an Elf took his life."

Fima spoke gently to Kino then, for he knew that the future of the Company depended on it. "I am thankful that Grundin's folk brought his remains to you, and we share your grief, for we also lost a friend to this creature. Gorgon tried to bring the suspicion upon Gaelen of the Greatwood, but Lord Grundin saw through this effort, and thus it was fruitless. I do know that Nimo was not convinced, for he hated Gaelen even before Gorgon worked his evil. I would hope that you are more enlightened, Kino. Still, the metal gains some of its character from the mine where it was delved. Will you hear our defense of the Elf, or no? If you will, then Rogond and I shall tell you the tale from the beginning. All we ask is leave to go on our way in search of Belko."

The old dwarf rested his chin in his right hand as he considered. The Company was asking a lot of him—to put aside thousands of years of mistrust and accept the tale of strangers, allowing them to walk free. Yet there was a glimmer of doubt in his eyes...perhaps Nimo had been mistaken? It couldn't hurt to hear the tale.

Then the one standing at Kino's right hand spoke quietly to him. "Noli was my cousin, as is Nimo, Most Honored Lord. Do not be persuaded by these honeyed words, spoken by one who has forgotten his place while languishing in Mountain-home. What will your people say if you are beguiled? You must make an example of these strangers. Lock them up, and do not listen to their lies. Perhaps they can deliver this "Gaelen" to you, and then you may hear from her and decide her fate. Noli may then be avenged, and rest more easily in the deeps of the Harnian. Lock them up, and do not speak to them again until they tell you where she may be found. See if they are willing to allow you to examine her for yourself. Let her prove her innocence, if any exists!"

Kino raised his head from his hand and looked hard at Fima and Rogond, whose unhappy expressions indicated that they had overheard. "What say you to this plan? Will you aid us in finding and bringing this Elf before me? You said you left her behind, therefore you know where she may be found. Will you aid me in learning the truth from her?"

Rogond's eyes widened as he looked over at Fima. Gaelen would surely be killed if she stood before Kino and failed to convince him of her innocence. "What will you do to her, if you do not believe her tale?" asked Rogond, looking into Kino's dark, glittering eyes.

"She will be slain, Aridan. That much you knew already. You think I would allow the one who took my son to draw breath? Still, should that come to pass, I promise I will kill her quickly and she will not suffer. She showed Noli the same courtesy. His death was quick, and she was not cruel to him."

"She did not *kill* him! You speak as though you are already convinced of her guilt!" cried Fima.

"Indeed," said Rogond softly. "I had thought you wise, but now I fear I must decline, though I face your wrath, for I am uncertain. I will not betray Gaelen even to save the Company. You will have to find another way."

Kino's eyes flashed. "You ask favors of me, and yet will give nothing back? I will lock you both up and allow you to languish here until you reconsider my request. After a few weeks of solitude with only bread and water, you may relent. And I will not listen to any more of your tales, for in your estimation I am not wise enough to comprehend them."

He rose and turned to the guards that stood by the door. "Take them back to their cells, and give them neither light nor sustenance. Deprive the others as well, if you have not already done so." As Rogond and Fima were led away he called after them:

"Since you claim to seek Belko, you should know that he is dead. His realm is beset by enemies, and you seek him in vain. I'm certain you did not take this into your plan. Now go, and consider what you have heard. When you are ready to be reasonable, I will hear you again."

"Belko dead? His realm beleaguered?" said Fima. "Why have your folk not rallied to his aid?"

"That is none of your affair," said Kino.

"Your smoldering gaze warns of many truths, and I sense you're not proud of them," said Fima. He shook his head sadly. "You are not leaving this Aridan with a very high estimation of the clan of Rûmm. If you think that we will turn upon the Elf, you will have a very long wait before you hear from us again. I'm sorry about Noli, but even sorrier that you cannot seem to rise above your hatred long enough to hear the truth of his death. Farewell. If you come to your senses, you will know where I am."

"That I will, indeed," said Kino, his eyes as hard as the stone of the dark prison in which Rogond and Fima again found themselves, both wondering what would become of them, and what Gaelen would do when they did not return.

Gaelen learned many things as Noro, Feori and Kari escorted her into the depths of the mountain. They were brothers, kin to Belko and Beori, whose clan had been founded by dwarves of the Deep-caverns. They got along well enough with Kino and his folk, but lately the two clans had been estranged, and rarely encountered one another. "Kino's heart has hardened since the death of his wife, and even more at the loss of his eldest son and heir. He has withdrawn into his own realm, shutting out the other clans in his grief," said Kari. "We regret this estrangement, for we have always tried to keep out of the disputes between the Elves and Kino's folk. Our own great craftsmen were once quite friendly with Elves, hence the seven-rayed stars of the Èolar are still featured in the insignias of our houses."

The dwarves guided Gaelen swiftly and well, turning expertly through the maze of passages. She tried to keep track of them, but was distracted and soon gave it up. At last they came to a passage that was well lighted, but had obviously not been well used in some time.

Noro explained that the dwarves had recently been forced to take new ways into their domain, as the old ones had been blocked or were under watch by their enemies. He trotted along the passage, then made one more turn into what appeared to be a blind alcove. He faced the wall, shaking his head. "This is a difficult time for us, but our spirits are undaunted. We'll soon reclaim our domain. Ah! Here is the way into the sanctuary."

He pressed his hand against the stone, and another hidden doorway appeared. Gaelen marveled at how adept these folk were at hiding things with clever devices. The Elves also kept their great Realms hidden, but it was said that there was magic in them, rather than cleverness. Elves made many beautiful and useful things, but they did not possess the sheer cunning of the Rûmhar.

In a short while, Gaelen stood amidst a large group of dwarves in what appeared to be a rather makeshift hall. They regarded her with both curiosity and suspicion, which, of course, she had expected. Noro spoke urgently to an older dwarf, who departed and then reappeared after several minutes. "Belko's heir will be with you soon," he said. "Please sit and take food and drink until then."

The dwarves brought Gaelen a bowl of rich, savory stew and a large chunk of bread, as well as a flagon of water. She ate politely, bowing before them, thankful for the opportunity. The dwarves, many of whom had not yet set their eyes upon an Elf, watched her with interest. She had surrendered her weapons, and was no threat to them. When she thanked them graciously in their own tongue, many started back as though shocked.

"Oho, my good friends, we must guard our speech before this Elf, who knows our tongue! Betray no secrets before her!" They chuckled, and Gaelen relaxed. Hopefully, Belko's heir would hear her request, and she would be allowed to speak to Belko himself.

Noro and Feori sat beside her until they were called for, then they escorted her into an antechamber in which an obviously important dwarf with a very dark red beard sat upon a raised platform, surrounded by attendants. Gaelen did not need to be introduced, for his manner said all that was needed. She approached, and knelt before him. "Am I addressing Beori of the Harnian?"

"You are," said the dwarf. State your business, for we have pressing matters to attend to."

"I know of your difficulties," said Gaelen. "I am Taldin of the Greatwood Realm, and I bow humbly before you. I come to request aid, and to offer it. Will you hear me?"

Beori raised both eyebrows. Gaelen had spoken the Dwarf-tongue, and done it reasonably well. She did not yet know it, but Fima's insistence that she learn proper diction had aided her greatly in that hour. Beori bade her rise to her feet, saying, "Indeed, Taldin of the Woodland, I will hear your tale. What is your business in the Harnian?"

Gaelen looked levelly at him. She read no malice in his deep blue eyes, though there was some suspicion and mistrust there. She would need to dispel the doubts she saw in him, for she needed his aid. Taking a deep breath and squaring her shoulders, she began her tale. She told of seeking Belko to learn more of Hallagond, of discovering the ruined guard-chamber, and being redirected into the Realm of Kino, where her friends had been taken captive. She told Beori that they were now imprisoned for the slaying of Noli, though she failed to mention that she was, in fact, the very Elf accused of that act. *I don't need to tell him that…not yet.* When she had finished, Beori sat before her in silence, considering what he had heard.

"Why were you not also taken captive with your friends?" he asked.

"I was not with them. They felt it was wise to leave me behind, because they feared my presence might anger the dwarves. I once earned the wrath of Nimo, their kinsman, when I was in Cós-domhain."

"Did you, now?" said Beori with a wry look. "I've met Nimo. It would be easy to earn his wrath, so I will not inquire as to how you accomplished it. Yet I sense you're not telling everything you know, Taldin. Noro has informed me that you are Dwarf-friend in Grundin's Realm, and that you were seeking the aid of Belko. Would you now want to be taken to him?"

Gaelen nodded, though there was something unsettling in Beori's manner. In a few moments she knew the cause, for she was led into a burial-chamber, where a stately dwarf with the same long, red beard lay in a tomb of stone. He was richly dressed, and his polished armor gleamed, but Gaelen could still smell trolls all over him. She had failed to notice that Beori's beard had been torn, and cursed her inattentiveness. She turned to Beori, noting the tears standing in his eyes, and bowed her head.

"This is an ill fate, Beori son of Belko! I sorrow for your loss." Gaelen, of course, had no beard, but she thought quickly and tore out a small lock of her own hair, approached Belko's tomb, and laid it at his feet. Beori appreciated the gesture, for his face softened as he looked upon her.

"You have the gift of grace, Taldin of the Greatwood. I will go to Kino and try to convince him to release your friends, though I must tell you that my father had distanced us from Kino's clan of late. We aren't exactly at war, but we're getting there. It may be more difficult than I expect. Kino and his people have held no trust of the Elves, and they have always regarded our friendship with your people as suspect."

Gaelen wondered what had estranged them almost to the point of war, but thought better than to ask. She bowed before Beori. "My thanks. Even now your sire looks upon you with pride. If you will do this, and secure the release of my friends, I will offer their aid and mine in return. We will help you to rid your domain of this enemy that has driven you from it, and avenge Belko. Though I am certain that your folk are quite capable, it never hurts to have more warriors at your side."

Beori then called his folk together, and chose a delegation to accompany him to Kino's Hall. Gaelen would follow, but at a distance, as she did not wish to be seen by Kino or any of his folk. In that unfortunate event, Beori's people would know her as "Taldin," which would hopefully mean nothing to the dwarves of Kino's clan.

Just before they set out, Gaelen drew Beori aside. "When I mentioned the name of Hallagond, you nodded," she said. "Does this mean that you have knowledge of him?"

"He was well known to us, Taldin. But if your friend the Aridan seeks him, he will need to travel far away to the Eastern Hills, for that is where we last knew him to be. He also mentioned going south, perhaps to the great desert wastes, where no one would know his name. It's a sad tale, and I will say no more at present."

Gaelen's face fell as she heard Beori's words. It sounded as though Rogond would be in for disappointment again. Though the Eastern Hills were far away, the Company could easily reach them if they could gain their freedom from Kino and, of course, provided they did not all perish at the hands of trolls. Perhaps she should not have so quickly offered Beori aid in driving out his enemies, but Gaelen knew enough of dwarves to know that they would expect some aid in return for their own. It was always better to offer before being asked, and it was partly for this reason that Beori respected her.

Chapter 5

For a while, Gaelen walked ahead with Beori and his delegation. It was then that she learned of their troubles, and why they had been driven forth from their Great Hall. When she had offered to aid them she had expected a tale of ordinary trolls, but now, as she listened to Beori and his folk describing their enemies, she wondered. It was true that all trolls were evil, unintelligent, very large, and difficult to bring down. Their hides were thick, tough and scaly, and their skulls impenetrable. An archer could kill them only by shooting them directly in the eye or the mouth.

Gaelen wondered about these trolls in particular, as they seemed unusual in several ways. Perhaps the dwarves exaggerated, for the trolls surely were not as large as described. After all, they probably just looked larger to folk of such short stature. Yet these seemed also to be more adept, swifter and better organized than any trolls of Gaelen's admittedly limited acquaintance.

One thing was certain: as with most trolls, these loved and coveted treasure. They had now occupied the Great Hall and the treasure-room of Beori's clan. Though it probably would not compare favorably with the great treasure stores of Lord Grundin's realm, it would still be an impressive collection, no doubt featuring many beautiful and valuable items.

Though Belko and his folk had defended themselves with valor, they had been forced from their domain. Belko had been slain in an attempt to re-take the Great Hall, which would prove to be very difficult as there was now only one entrance—the trolls had blocked all others. This was going to take some planning.

"Forgive me, Beori, but have you sought the aid of the other clans in this? They must surely realize the same fate awaits them," said Gaelen. "You have said that there is strife between you. I do not intend to be so bold, but I would like to understand the nature of the waters into which I am about to throw myself, if you take my meaning."

Beori looked up at her as he strode along, his bushy red eyebrows raised. "You are bold, Taldin, but I suppose I can't blame you. The truth is that Kino and my father had been allies, but were estranged of late. It began with a dispute over which of our clans had discovered a rich lode of ore, and which of us has the right to mine it. Unfortunately, things got out of hand, and folk of both clans were killed. It didn't help matters when Lord Belko refused to trade a beautiful green gem that Kino covets. He taunted Kino, saying he would mount the gem and give it to the Elvenking in the Greatwood. He was only jesting, but Kino took it as a personal affront. Now we have vowed that we'll not rest until the ore deposit is ours, and Kino has done the same."

"People *died* for that? Why can you not simply share it?" Gaelen, who had little in the way of possessions, did not understand the lust in the hearts of dwarves for gems and bright metals.

Beori chuckled. "How little you appreciate what you're asking, Elf of Greatwood! You may not understand our folk as well as I thought if you think we can so easily share things that are precious to us. Kino's clan and mine are not so closely related that we can so easily settle such a dispute. Besides, there is more to it than that. Once Kino learned his son was killed by an Elf, his enmity toward us grew even greater. He demanded that we strike the stars from our insignia, calling us Elf-friends. With all due respect to your people, there is no greater crime in Kino's mind. The ore-deposit is just an excuse for the real enmity he holds for us."

"I see the stars remain on your insignia," said Gaelen. "Still, the dispute may need to be settled quickly, for these enemies may be beyond your folk and mine together. If so, we will need Kino and his clan."

"All things will fall as they are destined, and the future is unseen, Taldin. We'll see," said Beori. "But it would be best if Kino did not know that you are with us, at least not yet."

That's an understatement, thought Gaelen. "Don't worry," she said. "I won't tell them. My mother drowned all of her stupid children." Beori smiled, and they spoke no more to one another until they reached the borders of Kino's domain.

Gaelen said farewell to Beori and lingered back behind the dwarves, such that Kino's sentinels did not detect her. They escorted Beori's delegation to the Great Hall, and Gaelen once again found herself observing from her shadowy perch. When Beori and his contingent entered the Hall, the enmity from both clans was palpable.

"Hail, Kino, son of Kodo," said Beori, as all his folk bowed low. "We are here on behalf of a group of strangers who passed into your realm seeking my father's counsel, and who are now imprisoned. We would like to parley for their release into our custody, for their business was with our folk, and we would relieve you of the trouble of dealing with them."

Kino lifted his chin. "I don't know how you came to discover this," he said, "but I will know it ere long. It may interest you to learn that these strangers were traveling with the She-elf that killed my son. I have no intention of releasing them until she is handed over to us, so that we may determine her guilt. You're wasting your breath."

"Fima, the Lore-master of Mountain-home, also travels with them, if I am not mistaken," Beori replied. "He is our kin. Are you saying that you would keep him in prison, though his only crime was traveling with a She-elf?"

Kino's eyes grew colder. "Your beard is torn, Beori. We heard about Belko's death at the hands of your enemies. We also know that you have been driven from your realm. Have you no more important concerns than securing the release of Elves and Elf-friends? Ah, but I had forgotten—you are an Elf-friend yourself! And where is your father's blood-stone? I should think it would have passed to you."

"You can imagine where it is," growled Beori.

"Ah, of course, undoubtedly it's now part of a troll's hoard. The Blood-stone Clan with no blood-stone? Such a pity…though you still have those wretched Elvish stars to call your own. I would have thought you would be here begging for our aid, and perhaps offering give over the new ore-lode that our people rightly claim. After all, it should be mined by 70 dwarves, not by those whose clan crest bears the stain of Elves. Yet, to my surprise, I see that you would come asking favors of us, and offering nothing in return. Give me one reason why we should grant your request, and I will consider it."

Beori thought for a moment. "Will you tell me of the strangers first, that I may understand why they are imprisoned?" Kino nodded, and told Beori the tale.

"So they are in prison because they will not betray this 'Gaelen' to you?" asked Beori, when Kino had finished.

"They are in prison because they will not bring this Elf before me that her guilt may be judged. They claim she is innocent, yet they will not allow us to decide for ourselves. Because we cannot judge for ourselves, we must assume her guilt. As such, if we cannot take her life in payment, the lives of her companions are forfeit. I will grant them time to consider, but I will not wait forever. Noli's blood cries out to me from the deeps. I know that he was slain without cause, and I would avenge him. You will never convince me otherwise!"

Kino's voice rose almost into hysteria, his eyes glittering under hoary white eyebrows. "Now that you have heard the tale, can you give me a single reason why I should grant your request and release the strangers?"

Beori glowered back at him, though he knew he had to be careful. Kino's temperament was tricky at best, especially lately. "You will not harm Fima son of Khima while any of our folk draw breath, of that I am certain. He is our kinsman. At least bring him here, so that he may account for himself."

"Why should I? What will you do to me if I don't?" said Kino.

"I will wonder how the venerable and respected sire of a fine dwarf like Noli became so ill-mannered all of a sudden," said Beori. "Since his courtesy was unimpeachable in times past."

This seemed to affect Kino, and he motioned to his attendants. "They will fetch the lap-dog of Ordath," he said. "Have no fear."

Gaelen listened from the dark ledge, keeping out of the light, trying to understand as much of what was said as she could. She had not known of Kino's demand that the Company betray her, and she listened in horror to the declaration that their lives would be forfeit if they did not deliver her to be judged. She watched as Fima was brought before Kino. Beori greeted him as a kinsman, though they had not met before.

Kino cast a suspicious glance at Fima. "I was not aware that you were such close kin, Beori. Pray explain the nature of your relationship."

"We are not exactly close kin," said Beori. "Fima is my distant cousin on his mother's side, but he has gained renown as a lore-master, and he sat upon the Council of Elders in the Deep-cavern realm. He is worthy of respect."

Fima bowed low in acknowledgment of this praise, as Beori then turned to him: "How came you to be among these strangers, Fima Lore-master? Why do you seek Belko's aid? And what of Kino's claim that the She-elf traveling with you is the slayer of Noli?"

Fima drew a deep breath, and then answered Beori's questions, his blue eyes never wavering, his voice steady and calm.

"Though we could not account for her whereabouts at the time Noli was slain, Gaelen could not have killed him. She had been throttled nearly to death, and could neither speak nor move her head upon her neck. She was bruised and torn, and barely alive...she had taken these injuries while trying to defend one of our comrades. We believed at the time that the creature, Gorgon Elfhunter, thought he had killed her, and thus left her for dead. I was also there when Lord Grundin questioned her. She was quite shocked to learn of Noli's death, and, though she held no great love for him, there was sadness in her eyes. She did not kill him, despite Nimo's refusal to see it. Grundin named her Dwarf-friend because she placed the well-being of his folk before her own."

"Did he, indeed?" said Beori, who was beginning to realize that the Elf in question was no doubt watching them at this very moment. "Tell me, Fima, what does this She-elf look like? A rather smallish Elf with unusually cropped hair has already come before me seeking aid from Belko. She gave her name as 'Taldin,' and she has proven that she is Dwarf-friend." He looked at Fima knowingly. "She speaks our tongue rather well."

Fima's expression did not waver, but in that moment he knew that Gaelen had disobeyed, and had gone into the mountain.

"And where is this Elf, Beori?" said Kino. "You had best tell us if you would not start a war, here and now!"

Beori grew stern and drew himself up tall, as Fima stood beside him, still bound. Beori's folk clustered behind him like a protective wall, but they were vastly outnumbered, and things would not go well for them should the tension erupt into strife.

69

"Until I am assured that you will be reasonable, I cannot say," said Beori. "She is a guest among my folk, and has given me no reason to suspect her of anything. In addition, she has promised her aid, and that of her companions, in ridding our domain of our foes…which is more than you have offered to do!"

"I offered aid to your father, and you *know* it!"

"But we could not afford the price of your aid, and the offer came far too late," said Beori, his teeth and his fists clenched. "And *you* know it!"

Kino rose to his feet. Many of his folk were muttering angrily. Things were not going well.

As Gaelen watched from above, it seemed that there was only one course of action open to her. Unlike Rogond, who would spend precious time in consideration of alternatives, Gaelen would act quickly. She stood upon the ledge and stepped into the light, but the dwarves did not appear to notice, as they were focused on their own conflict. She drew her bow and sent a swift arrow straight into the back of the oaken chair inches above Kino's head, where it quivered dramatically.

For a moment, no one moved. All eyes were drawn to Gaelen as she cried out in the dwarf-tongue: "If you want Gaelen Taldin, here I am! I surrender to you." She threw her bow, quiver, short sword, and long knives down at the feet of the astonished dwarves, then leaped from the ledge, landing first upon one of the great oaken beams spanning the hall, and then onto the floor directly in front of Kino. The dwarves rushed forward, Beori's folk surrounded her before they could take her.

Kino stood and held up his hand. "Let her speak, and explain herself to us. She is now unarmed. Yet bind her first…I will not breathe easily until she is rendered harmless." He reached up behind his head, extracting the arrow from the chair with some difficulty. "I know that you could have killed me, yet you did not. Therefore, I will hear you."

"Hear me, then," said Gaelen, "for I grow weary of trying to understand your debate. I would protect not only my friends, but Beori, who needs your aid, not your enmity. I will not come between the clans, but neither will I suffer myself to be bound. You have my promise that I will raise no hand or weapon to you, and that must suffice."

Kino took note of the archers now positioned on all sides of the hall. They would drop her in a heartbeat at a sign from him.

"Very well, so be it. What have you to say?"

"Only this: I did not kill Noli. A monstrous creature named Gorgon Elfhunter did that. He also killed my friend Belegund, and another dwarf named Tibo, to say nothing of the many, many Elves whose lives have ended unspeakably at his hands. He still lives, to my great sorrow. I have sworn that I will not rest until he is dead, and his victims avenged. Kill me, and you kill one of your greatest allies in accomplishing Noli's vengeance."

She fell silent, watching Kino's lined, weathered face.

"She's right, Kino," said Fima. "I know Gaelen well, and she will not rest until Gorgon is brought low. I believe in my heart that she is destined to do so."

"She is Dwarf-friend," said Beori. "Remember, Kino—Lord Grundin placed great trust in her to have bestowed such an honor. She is Dwarf-friend! Ask her to show you the proof." Kino's folk clamored in agreement, for they respected Lord Grundin. If Gaelen could prove herself to be Dwarf-friend, at least some of them would view her differently.

"Very well," said Kino. "Show me the proof that you are Dwarf-friend."

Gaelen shrugged, then sat down upon the polished stone floor and removed one of her boots. She reached up under the leg of her leather breeches and extracted a small golden medallion, gave it a quick polish using the sleeve of her tunic, rose to her feet and handed it to Kino, looking him calmly in the eye.

When Kino examined the medallion, his eyes grew wide. He showed it to the dwarf standing at his right hand—the one who had spoken against the Company earlier. Now he was silent.

"May I see that, please?" asked Fima. He received the small golden token, looked closely at it, and smiled. "Hear me, all Ye Dwarves," he said. "This token is one of the original pieces that came from the ancient treasure-stores of the Five Founders, and was made with their own hands when they were first learning the craft of metal-smithy. Can you see the markings?"

He handed it back to Gaelen. "This is rare and very special. Guard it well…it dates from the beginning of the First Reckoning—from the very emergence of my people in this world."

Gaelen took the token reverently, replacing it with care.

"You have earned the trust of Lord Grundin, and are Dwarf-friend," said Kino, as Gaelen faced him once more. "Though it pains me to say, it is possible that Nimo has misjudged you. You could have killed me, and did not. You surrendered yourself to our judgment, and that shall now be rendered. You are not our friend, Elf, and none of your kind shall ever be, but I no longer hold you guilty in the death of my son. Know, however, that I will hold you to your claim that you will seek vengeance upon his killer. I will now release the lot of you to the custody of Beori, son of Belko. Leave me now, for I will not wish to look upon any of you again."

"I thank you for your generosity, and for your willingness to admit my innocence in the face of overwhelming evidence," said Gaelen. "I would be only too happy to ensure that you never need look upon me again, but it's not that simple. Beori's folk face a terrible enemy. I am Dwarf-friend, and I stand ready to assist them…will you not also lend your aid? These enemies will also come for your domain, and your treasures. You should want to aid Beori's folk in getting rid of them, surely."

Dead silence fell in the Great Hall. Then Beori and his folk, who had stood open-mouthed at the suggestion that they needed this Elf to speak in their behalf, began to laugh. Gaelen flushed, though she did not drop her eyes from Kino's.

Fima winced, and stepped forward quickly. "Forgive her impertinence, my Lord Kino. As with many of her folk, she does not know when to keep silent! We thank you for your generous and just decision, and will be on our way as quickly as we may."

He turned to Gaelen, and snapped at her in the Elven-speech. "For the love of heaven, control your tongue! You do not know how difficult this is for him. Take your life, and your friends, and depart from his halls. Do not look for aid from his folk. Apparently you have sworn us all in service to Beori, whom you just came perilously close to insulting. We will just have to make do with what we have. This may yet end badly!"

Gaelen was chastened, and she bowed before Kino, but she could not entirely keep silent. "It is a difference between our races, Fima, that your people will place things like gold and gems above the lives of their kin, however distant." She turned and followed Beori out of the Hall. If Kino heard her, he gave no sign.

Chapter 6

The Company was reunited within the hour, to their great relief. They were let out of their cells, blinking and shielding their eyes from the light, for they had been in near-total darkness for many hours. The dwarves who released them did so grudgingly; some of them had been looking forward to keeping their captives uncomfortable for a long time. Gaelen's friends were somewhat surprised to see her, especially Rogond, who didn't know whether to be overjoyed or furious.

"Why can you not do as you are told, *ever*? At least you are reliably disobedient! You are very lucky to be alive, Gaelen. One day your luck will run out, and you'll wish that you had listened to someone else for a change. It's a good thing Fima was there to assist you."

Gaelen regarded him in silence, her arms folded, her expression cool. Fima shuffled his feet and looked uncomfortable. "Errr… Rogond, you might want to hear the tale first," he said.

"Indeed, I'm sure I will," said Rogond, "but not just now." He turned back to Gaelen. "You betrayed your promise to me, Gaelen—I don't know whether I should ever trust you again. I probably should not be dealing with you right now, as I'm angry. But you deliberately disobeyed and placed yourself in grave peril! Do you have any *idea* what they would have done to you if whatever undoubtedly reckless chance you took had not succeeded? You will turn my hair grey before my time." The flush of his cheeks could be clearly seen, even through his stubbly beard, and his eyes were bright with emotion. He turned back to Fima. "I'm going to regret this outburst later, aren't I?" Fima simply shrugged.

"Go and calm yourself, Rogond," said Gaelen, "so that we may speak further of this when you are more rational. You made me promise to remain, and I did…for a while. Then I did the only thing I could do—I protected you.. Next time I will remain with the horses, and wonder what became of my friends as they sit languishing in dark cells while hostile dwarves discuss how they might best be slain."

Beori strode up to Gaelen, not realizing that he was interrupting. "Worthy Elf, your friends have been released, and you are at our service now, as we agreed. Let's go and lay plans to reclaim our own. We're thankful to have your aid, for this will be a daunting task. Let's hope that we all come through it in the end. Follow me."

Galador looked after him. "What was that about?" He looked over at Gaelen, who was now looking down at the floor. "You have obviously promised him something, Gaelen, and I'm not certain I cared for his reference to a 'daunting task.'"

Fima shook his head, for he already knew of Gaelen's promise. "You have no idea."

Rogond then rounded on Gaelen before he left. "Oh, I cannot *wait* to hear what you have promised him, though I've seen just lately what a promise from you is worth. I'm sure it involves something extremely hazardous. You are…you are *exasperating!* You could have been taken from me. I…I cannot speak of this now." He turned and strode away, muttering under his breath, gesturing with both hands. Fima looked after him, then turned back to regard the rather confused faces of Galador and Nelwyn. His expression softened in a knowing smile.

"He is in love."

Gaelen and Rogond would not speak to each other as they followed Beori's folk back to their temporary stronghold. As he walked along, Fima tried to tell as much of the tale as he knew. Nelwyn did nothing for Rogond's mood, as she was terribly impressed with her cousin's fortitude, and praised her for her resourcefulness.

Galador tried to mollify Rogond. "Don't worry, my friend. I know Gaelen acted rashly, but she did prevail—even you will have to admit she was resourceful. She figured out the secret of the doorway, even as you did, and she apparently impressed Beori enough that he came to her aid. Be calm, my friend. All is well for the moment."

Rogond's expression was stony as he strode slowly along with the bustling dwarves. "One of these times, she is going to be too clever and too resourceful for her own good. Then I shall lose her."

"Ah, yes, but it might be wise for you to remember why you love her in the first place," said Galador. "Ask yourself, would you really change anything about her?"

Rogond wondered. Would he change anything about Gaelen? "Perhaps I would arrange it so that she would keep her promises to me for more than an hour or two," he muttered. But that was only part of what was bothering him...it seemed that Gaelen did not trust him to take care of himself. And this time, to his humiliation, she had been right. *Damn her eyes...*

Galador clapped him on the shoulder. "I do not envy you, my friend. I'm quite happy with my gentle, sensible Nelwyn. Yet there is much to admire in Gaelen. I wish you the best of luck."

"*Sensible*, am I?" Nelwyn had come up behind Galador, and had overheard. "I can think of many names I would rather be given."

"Of course, my love," replied Galador, smiling at her. "Beautiful, wise, winsome Nelwyn, in whose eyes the star of my heart shines forever, and in whose golden hair the sunlight of my very soul resides...is that more to your liking?"

Rogond chuckled, as Nelwyn favored Galador with a wry look. "Quite the wordsmith, aren't you?" Galador did not reply, but only smiled at her.

Fima stalked up behind them, shaking his head. "Rogond, I know you are angry with Gaelen for breaking her promise, but there's something you have to understand. She made a stone vow when she gave her heart to you in Mountain-home, and that vow can never be broken. She could not do what you asked...do you understand?"

"No," said Rogond. "I don't. She promised to remain and she broke that promise; I'm thinking she let it remain for only a few hours, if that. I feel betrayed, and it hurts my soul that her promise would be worth so little, or that she would have so little faith in me."

"She has lived for so long on her own that it's difficult for her to have faith in others when she sees them heading down a dangerous road," said Fima. "Hunter-scouts protect and defend, and she has

77

been doing that for a thousand years. You asked too much of her." He paused for a moment, considering. "Ordinary promises are easily broken, and Gaelen does not make them. She makes iron promises…they are strong, but will bend when heated too much. This one bent in the fires of the vow she made in Mountain-home… the stone vow. Iron breaks upon stone, you know. She cannot keep one promise if it means breaking another, stronger one. She tried to tell you that."

"If she knew the iron would break, she should not have made the promise," said Rogond. "Why are you taking up for her, anyway?"

Fima shrugged. "Because I understand why she did what she did. Gaelen is utterly predictable, you know. She followed to protect you, but not close enough to endanger you. I'll say one thing—the little menace has an uncanny talent for landing on her feet. This could have gone so very, very badly…"

"We have yet to hear how badly it may have gone," Rogond reminded him. "I wonder what kind of promise she made to Beori? Let's hope it was of iron, and not of stone." He shook his head. "What nonsense!"

"Call it nonsense if you will, Rogond. I'm sorry you don't care for my little comparison. But I'd suggest you abandon your black mood for now, as we're approaching Beori's stronghold, and we'll need our good humor. These enemies are formidable; they have driven forth a doughty clan of dwarves, and will not be easily routed, but make no mistake—if Gaelen had not offered to aid Beori she would have received little aid from him, and you would probably still be brooding in your dark cells with little hope of release. We should all be at least a little grateful for her disobedience."

Rogond nodded. "We have not yet heard the full tale, Fima. I'll reserve judgment until then."

Fima chuckled. "Very fair and predictable of you, Rogond. I look forward to telling you the tale, with Gaelen's aid. Even I do not know all of it as yet. Ah! Here we are."

Beori's folk directed them inside the makeshift hall, where many of the dwarves were already assembled. Beori himself stood once more upon the raised platform, addressing them all in his deep, throaty growl.

"My people, these strangers have offered to aid us in reclaiming our domain. The time has come for us to drive the darkness from our halls, and avenge the blood of Belko. No doubt many of us will give our lives in this cause, but it is one worth fighting for, and we shall see it done!" At this, many of the dwarves cheered. "We will refresh our guests with food and drink, for they have a difficult task before them. I have been assured that they are formidable warriors, and will be a match for our fearsome enemies. May their bows and blades soon lead to the downfall of the Trolls of D'hanar!" There was more cheering, louder this time.

D'hanar? mouthed Rogond at Thorndil, who had turned quite pale. No northern Ranger has ever heard that name without dread. D'hanar was the dwarves' name for the lands near to the ruin of Tal-elathas. Lord Wrothgar had kept his stronghold there, and had dwelt there himself until the Third Battle. His most trusted and evil servant, the dark Asarla Lord Kotos, had dwelt there also.

Very, very evil things were spawned in those lands. Trolls of D'hanar would no doubt be among the worst. Gaelen and Nelwyn, who knew little of this save what they had heard in tales, appeared surprised but undaunted. Fima and Galador, on the other hand, knew better, and their faces showed it. When the dwarves came to offer them all food and drink, they had little appetite for either.

Beori joined them. "Not eating? I should have thought you would be quite hungry after your imprisonment. I know that Kino didn't give you much food or drink. Perhaps our fare is not to your liking?"

"There is nothing wrong with your food or your ale, my Lord Beori," said Fima. "My friends were unaware of Gaelen's promise, and have not yet grasped the full meaning of it."

"I see," said Beori, peering at them from under his eyebrows. "Well, I suppose I don't blame you. Yet the promise was made. I trust you will keep it?"

"Indeed," said Rogond, "in fact we are just thinking of ways in which we might accomplish it. Describe these trolls, my lord. How many are they, and how fierce?"

"There are six of them, and they are *very* fierce," said Beori. We lost over a hundred of our folk in the first attack, and nearly as many in the second, including Belko, my father." He cast his eyes down for a moment before continuing. "It will take all the force we have and a considerable measure of luck to defeat them. Yet our scouts reported three dead trolls out by the foothills to the southeast, and they had been slain with blades and Elvish arrows—your folk, I wonder?"

Gaelen and Nelwyn nodded. "We intended only to draw the trolls from the Company, but things went awry and we were forced to engage them," said Nelwyn.

"You killed three hill-trolls alone and unaided?" asked Beori in wonderment. Then his face split into a wide grin, just visible through his full, red beard. "I sense our troubles are over! There are only six of these, and though they are...somewhat more formidable than hill-trolls, they should pose little threat to such marksmen. This news has put me in quite a good humor—good enough to share the only bottle of truly magnificent wine remaining to us."

He hurried off to fetch it, as Gaelen looked optimistically at Rogond. "You see? Beori thinks these trolls will give little trouble, and we shall have all these dwarf-warriors standing with us."

But Fima was unconvinced. "How naïve you are! He sensed that you were all losing heart, and he made light of the task so that you would not, that's all. The test will be when he brings the wine— if he serves it to you in spite of what I say to him, then we are facing great peril. Watch closely."

Beori returned with the bottle of wine clutched lovingly in both hands like a precious jewel. Before he could open it, Fima tried to stay him. "Perhaps we should save that fine wine until after the victory, when we are all in your Great Hall toasting the defeat of your enemies! What say you?"

Beori looked wistfully ahead, as though thinking of how grand that moment would be. "No, my friends. I would rather drink now, and strengthen my courage, for the future is ever uncertain. That victory celebration will come soon enough." When he opened the bottle of wine—and it was indeed very fine—he poured some for each of them. They lifted their glasses in a toast to future victory, but all knew that the uncertain future Beori referred to might mean the deaths of one or of all.

Beori had convened a war-council, inviting everyone in the Company. When the dwarf who had been sent to collect them approached, he looked curiously at Rogond. "Do you know of a Ranger named Hallagond? It's my opinion that you resemble him, though I must admit that most men resemble one another in my eyes."

Rogond had smiled then, for he was surely on the right path to learn more. "Yes, Hallagond is my brother. But I know almost nothing of him, and have in fact sought out your folk that you might enlighten me. I'm searching for him, and would learn all I can."

The dwarf's eyes grew melancholy then, and he muttered something under his breath that Rogond could not hear. Then he spoke in a low voice. "Hallagond was a worthy man, and he was the friend of the Blood-stone Clan. He and his companions came to our aid on several occasions. Alas! I fear that you will be dismayed by what you learn, but there may be others here who know more of his tale than I."

Beori then approached, interrupting them. "You are needed at this war-council, Aridan. There will be time later for the telling of tales, should our plan succeed. If it does not, then it won't matter." He cast a meaningful look at the dwarf standing beside Rogond, who bowed low and took his leave.

Rogond's thoughts of his brother's fate turned with unpleasant swiftness in his mind, but he banished them for the time being. The Company would have need of clear thinking in order to make a successful plan.

Galador had already shown his usefulness, as he had aided in the defense of Eádros long ago, and had considerable experience. The Rangers were likewise helpful, as they had seen more than their share of trolls, though these six were not typical—they were much larger and more cunning. They wore primitive clothing, and even spoke a sort of primitive Aridani. Their hides were thicker as well, for the axes of the dwarves made little dent in them. They would need to be taken by archers, most probably. Hopefully they would still fall to an arrow in the eye.

Gaelen sat back through all this planning, listening to talk of storming the Great Hall and the treasure-rooms, the dwarves sacrificing themselves so that the archers could come within close range and fell the trolls quickly, and so on. She looked over at Nelwyn. "Do you recall our first encounter with Gorgon? How we defeated him? We had little hope of prevailing through strength at arms, yet there was one weapon he could not withstand, and these trolls will be the same. Why do we not use it?" She referred, of course, to sunlight, which no troll would tolerate—it would turn to stone immediately, and remain so forever after.

"Ummm…because we are underground?" Nelwyn replied, with a wry look at her cousin. "Or have you forgotten?"

"I have not forgotten. Yet there must be ways that the dwarves direct light from outside into the deeps. The Elven lamps cannot generate their own light; they can only capture it. Light that is captured can be added together and made stronger…I'm thinking mirrors and lenses, though I wouldn't have the slightest notion of how to use them. Why do we not see whether we can flood the chambers with *sunlight?* Then the trolls will be helpless. We can block them in, and they will then be forced to endure the light, and become stone."

She looked over at the war-council, where the dwarves, the Rangers, and Galador were pointing at the large map of Beori's domain spread before them, arguing and gesturing. Rogond sat back, slowly shaking his head, his expression telling that he was unhappy with what he was hearing. But he would always listen to Gaelen, and she moved to stand behind him, speaking softly into his ear. Nelwyn watched Rogond's face as Gaelen explained her idea, and his expression changed several times as he considered it. He turned and spoke to her in return. Then she returned to her place beside Nelwyn, and waited.

At last the Council grew silent, for they had reached an impasse. The present plan was uncertain at best, and it held great risk to all. All save Rogond sat with downcast eyes. The plan had taken a wrong turn, but they didn't know what to do about it, and they were weary. Rogond, however, was now bright and eager as he studied the map.

Gaelen smiled to herself. Rogond was very resourceful. She knew that he would craft a way to put her suggestion to use. He had been paying little attention to what had been said around him for quite some time now, for his thoughts were turning in a different direction.

"Perhaps we should eat, drink, and take rest before reconvening the council," said Beori. "I am weary, and I need to refresh my thinking." He yawned and stretched, as Fima and Thorndil nodded in agreement.

"Not yet, my friends," said Rogond eagerly. "Wait until you hear my thoughts. I must tell of them while they are still fresh, as they may leave me. There exists a weapon so powerful that it will vanquish the trolls at once, and all we need do is figure a way to bring it to your halls."

Galador sat up tall, for he knew his friend's idea would have merit. He looked over at Gaelen and Nelwyn, his expression hopeful. Gaelen mouthed a single word at him: *Solas.* Galador frowned as he considered, then lifted both his eyebrows and nodded in assent. Rogond would find a way.

"What is this weapon?" asked Beori with interest. All his folk were now completely focused on Rogond's next few words.

"Trolls turn back to the stone from which they are made should the light of the sun hit them. The weapon is sunlight. All we need is a way to bring it below ground, and a way to make certain the trolls are trapped within and cannot escape it. We will need to lure them into the trap, and that task will be the most perilous. Those chosen must be swift, agile, and skilled. The others need do only two tasks—block the trolls in, and make certain the sunlight reaches them."

Beori's face wore a blank expression as he stared back at Rogond. Then he frowned. "I thought you had come up with a plan that could actually work, Aridan. You definitely need rest and a good ration of ale...unless you have already been partaking of it unseen. With respect, this plan might have sprung from the mind of a drunken dwarf! We are deep beneath the mountainside, my friend, and you cannot bring the sun so far within." But some of the dwarves were muttering with excitement already, their busy minds turning.

"Do you not already make use of natural light through shafts and tunnels?" asked Rogond, who knew the truth of it. "And can light not be captured and reflected, and then directed? There is a way! Look here…"

For the next several minutes he explained his plan, pointing here and there at the map, as the council looked on in wonder.

"Aridan, I must admit that your plan is clever, and might actually succeed, yet our treasure-stores and armaments are taken by the trolls, and we have no devices to accomplish it. Our smithy is likewise overrun. How can we obtain what we need?"

Rogond looked hopefully at Fima. "Would the dwarves of Kino's clan have such items?"

"They will, and more could be made at need," said Fima. "But we should not even consider asking for help from Kino. It's enough that he released us unharmed."

"He will aid Beori," said Gaelen quietly, "if the right words are chosen." Then she rose and left them all to wonder as to her meaning. Fima and Beori followed her, after dismissing the council so that all could take food and drink. They found her sitting alone in a dark corner, her eyes calm and bright.

She inclined her head to Beori as he approached, then looked levelly at him, speaking in a soft, clear voice. "Your folk have endured terrible loss. Your realm has been overrun, and your people slain; your treasury and your smithies are lost to you. Even now, your enemies befoul them. Our worthy Aridan has given you a plan that will succeed, if only we have the necessary tools to accomplish it. Your lands will be reclaimed, and your treasures restored to you. Your mighty sire will be avenged, and your folk safeguarded. All we need is Kino's aid. Are these things not worth more than ore deposits?"

Fima drew in a long breath, stood back, and appraised Beori calmly. The Dwarf-lord stood still as stone, his face expressionless. Gaelen did not speak again, but rose to her feet, bowed, and took her leave. She had said all that was needed. Now it would be up to Beori to consider whether he could give up something so precious, and in his mind rightfully his, to Kino. Belko had vowed never to relinquish the new lode to Kino's grasping hands—Beori would also find this difficult. Dwarves often value their pride above life itself.

"Now we shall see what sort of leader he will make, and whether Belko's blood is of real quality," muttered Fima. He lingered for a moment before following Gaelen back toward the now-lively gathering of friends who lifted their tankards in greeting.

"What did you say to him?" asked Rogond as Fima and Gaelen approached.

Fima smiled. "Our Gaelen has given Beori a difficult choice, yet her words were well chosen. You have been a good influence on her, my friend."

Gaelen appeared not to notice as she sat beside Nelwyn. She politely declined the offer of ale, for she had never been fond of it. She was tense, for she worried about the decision that Beori would make, and the fate of Rogond's plan.

The dwarves took notice, and they set many sorts of food and drink before her, hoping to tempt her. She tasted everything politely, praising its worth, but was still troubled. Then Nelwyn drew forth from under the table a no-longer-quite-full honey jar, setting it before her with great ceremony. "Be of good cheer, my friend! Tomorrow may never come, but soon we will not care." She dipped two fingers into the dark, wild honey in a most discourteous manner, then brought them to her mouth, where they disappeared abruptly.

Gaelen smiled. "Why, Nelwyn! What have you brought? It appears you've forgotten your manners, and I shall join you in forgetting mine, if only you will leave some of that for me..."

Galador shook his head, turning to Fima and Rogond. "They will be quite as merry as can be before long," he said. "We should all enjoy this time, for a difficult task awaits us.

"Speaking of being merry...for a people besieged by trolls, they're being quite free with what remains of their ale," said Fima, shaking his head. "I suppose they expect to either reclaim their stores, or...or never need to drink ale again."

"No doubt," said Galador. "I must admit, the plan is inspired, though I still have no idea as to how we will acquire what we need to accomplish it. The workings of your mind amaze me at times,

Rogond. I lift my tankard to you." He did so, draining the last of the ale, whereupon a full tankard appeared at his elbow as if by magic.

"Lift your tankard to Gaelen. She thought first of using the light," said Rogond.

Galador did not reply. He sat for a moment, and then he lifted his full tankard to the soon-to-be-very-silly Wood-elf sitting across the table from him, and drank long and deep.

Hours later, Rogond sat with Fima and Gaelen, smoking a long clay pipe he had borrowed from the dwarves, lost in his own thoughts. Fima was likewise drawing quietly on his own pipe, as the sweet aroma of pipe-smoke wafted enticingly around them. Elves do not partake of pipe-leaf, though Gaelen liked the smell of it. She had gotten so besotted with wild honey that she was now curled up beside Rogond in a deep sleep. Nelwyn was no doubt in a similar state, and this was rare for either of them, as Elves do not sleep in the manner of men unless they are grieving, healing, or, as in this case, recovering from the effects of overindulgence.

Gaelen sighed, drawing her legs up to her belly, rolling partway onto her back. Rogond reached down and absently stroked her hair, unconsciously attempting to smooth it into place. He looked down into her peaceful, serene face, with its flawless features, and smiled. The warmth of the smile gave way to a chill as he considered the fate that might await them all. The plan he had put forth was complex, and all parts would need to come together before they could attempt it. They would first need to design the system to bring the light to the hall, and then they would need to acquire the items necessary to set it into place. They would need to have a clear, bright day, and to determine when the sunlight on that part of the mountain was most bright.

Rogond had decided, after studying the map and conferring with the dwarves, that the best place to trap the trolls was a smallish chamber off the Great Hall. This had originally been a council-chamber, and there was an air shaft already in the ceiling. The chamber was large enough to accommodate all six trolls while still giving those set to lure them room to evade, yet it was small enough that the trolls would not be able to escape the light, for every corner would be flooded.

Those souls selected to lure the trolls would have to be able to do so without being killed, and they would have to succeed in getting them all in the chamber together. Then the dwarves would block them in, and signal those on the outside to turn the light upon them. Hopefully, those of the Company who were also blocked inside would be able to evade the trolls until the light took effect.

Rogond was uneasy as he thought of it. Gaelen and Nelwyn were logical choices, as the trolls would not be able to resist chasing them, and they were swift and agile as well as skilled with the bow. Nelwyn, in fact, might possibly take one or two of the trolls even before the advent of the light. Yet something might go awry...what if the plan did not work? In that event, Gaelen and Nelwyn would be blocked in a small chamber with angry trolls—trolls out of D'hanar! And that was another question: who could say whether these trolls, spawned in that evil realm, did not possess unique capabilities? What if they were unaffected by sunlight? It was not impossible. Rogond had learned to never become complacent, assuming that things would happen the way he expected them to. There were things in Alterra about which he knew nothing, about which he could not even speculate, and against which he had no hope of prevailing.

He turned to Fima, who was now looking rather intently at him as though he could sense Rogond's trepidation. "Try not to worry too much, Rogond," he said. "These trolls may be out of D'hanar, but I sense they are not so powerful, or no dwarf would yet dwell beneath these mountains. Your plan will prevail." He drew thoughtfully on his pipe. "It's not your destiny to die here, Aridan. Nor will it be mine, or Gaelen's. There will be a satisfactory ending, you'll see. Beori's folk are clever and steadfast. They won't fail us."

"I'm grateful that you place such trust in me," said Rogond. "Yet I am troubled. The simpler a plan is, the more likely it will succeed. This plan is not simple—there are many ways in which it could fail."

Fima waved a dismissive hand. "How little faith you have in yourself! Your plan really is quite simple. You just need to be certain that everyone is in the right place at the right time. When it is over,

Beori will probably lead you to Hallagond himself, if he can." Fima was silent for a moment, then looked over at Gaelen's contented form. "She will want the task of luring the trolls, you know. And I can think of no one better. She and Nelwyn will both be chosen."

"I know, Fima. Believe me, I have known since the plan was made. She will want this task, and she will think it's a game, but it's not. This is a game where she makes only a few of the rules...the rest will be made for her. And if the plan fails, she and Nelwyn will be lost."

"Yes, I should suppose they will be, therefore we must make certain that the plan does not fail, and above all else," said the dwarf, blowing sweet blue smoke through his white beard, "we must keep them both from the honey-jar."

Beori came to stand before Rogond and Fima a short while later, wanting to know exactly what items would be required. Rogond shook his head. "I'm not yet certain, and so we'll need your aid, Beori, in forming the plan. Let's do so at once," he said. He rose and left Gaelen still sleeping, after gently covering her with his cloak so she would not chill.

When all plans had been laid, it was decided that the Company would require several large glass lenses and a number of mirror-bright reflectors. These would be cunningly placed so that a single bright beam of sunlight hitting the top of the ventilation shaft could be magnified, focused, directed, refocused and redirected into the chamber, where the last reflector would scatter it throughout. This last reflector would need to be held in place, which would be among the most difficult tasks. It was decided that those set to lure the trolls into the chamber would carry it with them; with luck, the light would work quickly.

Beori took a delegation of his most trusted folk, and left to seek Kino's aid. He returned not long after with Kino's promise that he would receive all assistance needed, as well as many dwarves to aid him. Kino's craftsmen were even now working with some of Beori's folk to construct the finest lenses and mirrors. They were promised in two days' time. Beori did not mention mining rights, but Fima learned that he had relinquished them to Kino, and that nothing more should be said of it.

It was decided that Gaelen would spend time scouting the area, taking stock of the task. There was only one path leading back to that part of Beori's realm, and it was dark and narrow, but Gaelen managed to follow Noro, who guided her well. She wrinkled her nose as the stench of trolls grew stronger. Finally, the passage opened into a large, torch-lit chamber through a small hole in the wall. Gaelen barely fit through it, but she did, dropping lightly down onto the stone floor. She hid herself at once, for the rumble of heavy feet could be heard, and soon two of the largest trolls she had ever seen lumbered into the room.

They were enormous, with greenish-grey, scaly skin covered with wart-like knobs. They used the common-tongue, speaking to one another in deep, gravelly voices, and wore more clothing than was customary, but what dismayed Gaelen most were their eyes, small and piggish, but not blankly stupid as with most trolls—these held an evil intelligence behind them. These trolls were not clever, but they were much cleverer than most. A third, even larger, joined them. It hushed the first two, who were arguing about whose job it was to maintain the torches this time. The largest troll then looked suspiciously around the room, sniffing the air. "I smell something," it said. "Dunno what it is, but I don't think I like it!"

The others sniffed the air as well. "Dwarf, I'm thinkin'," said one.

The second troll brightened. "Ooh! Fresh dwarf, is it? Let's have a look then. I haven't had a good, juicy-red meal in a while. Just the stuff in the cellars. Mind you, the ale's good..."

"How would there be dwarves here? We killed 'em all and drove the others into their dark holes. They can't get back in here," said the first. The third, largest troll cuffed him sharply, eliciting a howl of anger.

"Shut up an' listen! This ain't no dwarf, see! You know we always smell dwarf in here, anyway! This is somethin' else. I dunno what."

Gaelen, who crouched silently in her dark hiding place, wondered how in the world the trolls could detect any scent above their own reek, which even now hammered at her sensitive nose.

"Well, if you dunno what, then why worry about it?" asked the first troll. "Anyways, I'm hungry. I ain't gonna worry about no strange smells, not when I can be down in the larder fillin' my belly. You comin'?"

The troll that had caught Gaelen's scent looked all around, still sniffing. At last, it seemed satisfied. "Yeah, I'm comin'. Somebody needs to watch you, anyhow! You'll eat us out of our nice home, you will!" They shambled off, the largest one pausing for a moment and turning back, still sniffing. Then it shrugged and followed its fellows.

Gaelen was alone now, but she suddenly found she had lost all strength in her legs. If those trolls had decided to investigate her scent, they might have found her. She would have had a difficult time evading all three of them. She shuddered at the thought of what she would have to do to remain undetected, and went in search of a source of scent. It did not take long, as there was plenty to be had.

She made her way silently through the ruins of Belko's Realm. Beori had provided her with a map, which proved useful as she found the Great Hall and the adjoining council-room with ease. She encountered two other trolls there; the last was apparently in the treasury, where it liked to sit and paw endlessly through the dwarves' accumulation of wealth.

One of the trolls was sleeping, snoring so loudly that the entire hall resonated with the noise. Gaelen saw the entrance to the council-room, and she examined it carefully, wondering how the dwarves would accomplish the task of sealing it once the trolls were inside. She decided that her scouting mission would be far from complete if she did not go inside and survey the chamber.

She waited for a while, as the other troll sat contentedly on the floor, apparently playing some game with itself involving the dropping of rocks and sticks. Sort of like "Stones and bones," she thought. Her uncle Tarmagil had taught her, and she remembered teaching Wellyn when he was young, to the displeasure of his father, the King. The troll was so engrossed in the game that it didn't notice Gaelen as she slipped silently along in the shadows, hiding behind overturned tables, eventually reaching the entrance to the now dark council-chamber. Normally a shaft of fresh air and daylight shone dimly from the ceiling, but though she could see the shaft, it was probably blocked from above, and would need to be opened. She paced the chamber off, wondering how she and Nelwyn would evade six huge trolls in such a small space. Yet there were stone pillars to hide behind, some large chunks of broken stone here and there, and a fairly wide ledge about as high as the top of her head. She practiced springing up onto it, but she dislodged a small stone and it fell, rattling, to the floor.

For a moment, she did not dare to breathe, straining to hear the sounds in the Great Hall. Yet she heard only the deep, rumbling racket of the sleeping troll, and blessed her luck. She could probably drop a boulder and they would not notice, but best not to take chances. She dropped back down, still studying the shaft and the layout of the room, and finally turned to make her way back to the small hole in the wall, where Noro anxiously awaited her.

He was nearly beside himself. "Where have you been?" he hissed. "Those trolls came back in here, looking for whatever made that scent." He wrinkled his nose in distaste as she drew closer to him. "You have thoroughly disguised yourself, I see," he muttered. "At any rate, I'm surprised you missed them! Have you seen what you came to see?"

Gaelen nodded. She was satisfied, at least for the moment, but she would want to return later and learn more.

"Then let's be off, for I fear they are becoming suspicious," said Noro. "I don't wish to provide them with their next meal of fresh meat. Follow me."

While Gaelen was covering herself with troll-scent in the ruined hall, Nelwyn and Galador shared the much more attractive duty of surveying the air shaft from the outside. This took some time to get to, but they eventually were led there by Feori, who knew the area well. "Here is the opening," he said, indicating a plain but functional square stone platform with a hole in the center that had been covered by a large stone. "This is the source of light and fresh air for the council-chamber. The trolls have blocked it."

The three of them moved the heavy stone with considerable effort, so that light and air could filter down into the chamber again. "We will need to replace it before we leave, or they'll be suspicious," said Feori. "For now, we can look inside."

All Nelwyn could see was blackness, and all she could hear was the moaning "whoosh" of the air flowing through the long, dark passage. She shivered at the task before the dwarves; they would have to lower themselves into that tight passage and place the lenses and mirrors at the correct points. It was not inconceivable that they would get stuck, and be trapped there. A worse fate an Elf could not imagine.

Galador studied the sky, the angle of the sun, and the clouds. He was adept at interpreting what he read in the heavens, and what he felt in the air. "We're in for about another day of this," he mused, "but I sense the weather will clear then, and if I'm not mistaken, the sun will hit this part of the mountain best in late morning, just before noon. Am I correct, Noro?"

Noro shrugged. "Most probably you are, as I wasn't aware that your kind was ever mistaken." He chuckled good-naturedly at Galador, who scowled at him. "In truth, it's a good thing we'll have a day or two to make ready. Kino has promised to have the lenses by tomorrow—I'm just glad it won't be me who's carrying them down there! Let's go back now, so you can tell what you have seen." They moved the heavy stone back over the opening, cutting off the light again.

They returned to Beori's Hall to find Gaelen immersed in cold water from a clear spring that flowed through the rocks, attempting to wash away the troll-scent. The dwarves had obligingly taken her clothing and tended it; it was now drying before the fire. Gaelen climbed from the chill waters, shivering, and wrapped herself in Rogond's cloak that he had left for her.

That evening she sat with Beori, Noro and the rest of the Company, and told what she had seen. Nelwyn and Galador also told their tale, and the last of the plans were made. As soon as they could, the dwarves would place their devices in the shaft. Then, when the weather cleared and the sun rose high, they would carry out the plan.

There remained only two matters still to be decided. How would the dwarves accomplish the task of sealing the council-chamber with the trolls inside? Tomorrow Gaelen, Fima and Beori would venture there to investigate; a way would surely be found. And then, who would take the risk of luring the trolls into the chamber? Gaelen and Nelwyn stood forth first, for they were well suited to the task, and everyone knew it. Beori likewise wanted to go, for he was the leader of his clan now, and he would take the risk of defending them. Rogond wanted to go, but he and Thorndil would be needed to aid the dwarves in sealing the chamber. Galador stood last, saying that he would carry the large, heavy mirror that would scatter the light throughout the chamber. He would not allow Nelwyn to go without him. He would sound his horn when the trolls were in place, alerting those above to open the shaft, releasing the light. Then he would place the mirror, sealing the trolls' fate.

Thorndil was concerned, for these trolls were of an evil realm, and they might have powers as yet unknown. "What if they don't react to the sunlight? You will be trapped with them. Is there a way you can escape?"

Gaelen reassured him. "If they didn't react to light, would they have gone to all the trouble to block that tiny shaft from above? They must surely know that it's too small for their enemies to enter. I am not afraid," she stated simply.

"None will escape once we seal them in," replied Beori. "Not until the trolls are dead, one way or another. This must be agreed to by all, and accepted by those who put themselves at risk. You will have us ever in your debt should you succeed."

"We will succeed," said Rogond, even as he prayed it would be so. He wrapped his cloak around him. It smelled pleasantly like Gaelen, and he breathed deeply, taking courage from it.

When three more days had passed, they were ready. Gaelen, Fima and Beori had crept inside, surveyed the entrance to the chamber, and found that they could seal it by bringing down the two flanking pillars in the Great Hall. The stone of the roof would collapse, sealing the fate of those inside. "How will you accomplish that?" asked Gaelen, her eyes wide as she regarded the great pillars of rock.

"We built those pillars, Taldin," said Beori. "What we have made, we can unmake. Do not fear. Just look to your own concerns, for they are weighty enough!"

This was true. Gaelen, Nelwyn and Galador had to lure all six of the great, fierce trolls into the chamber. What if the trolls were too clever, and suspected a trap? In that event, not even three formidable Elves would withstand such foes for long, even with Beori to aid them.

Gaelen put all such thoughts from her mind. She could not afford to waver; her confidence and fortitude would be sorely needed. She knew that Rogond was unhappy leaving her side, but he was needed elsewhere. They could not risk too great a force inside the chamber, as the trolls might not like the odds and be reluctant to enter it. That would not do; the trolls had to believe that the Elves would be easily taken.

Gaelen planned to so enrage the trolls that they would chase her blindly into the council-chamber. She had this plan all laid out in her mind, and had shared it with Nelwyn and Galador. The first task was to make certain that all six trolls were together in pursuit of them, so Gaelen, as the undisputed master of the stealthy approach, would spirit herself through the realm until she had located all six. Then she would report back to Nelwyn and Galador, who would position themselves to intercept them. Gaelen would begin the task of luring them into position, picking up aid along the way from Nelwyn and finally Galador, who would first carry the heavy mirror to the chamber and conceal it. This part of the plan would be accomplished with little difficulty, for Gaelen and Nelwyn were quick and capable—even clever trolls would have difficulty catching them. Beori would go with Galador and watch over the mirror until the Elves fled into the chamber, pursued (hopefully) by their enemies.

The difficulty would come when they finally succeeded in trapping the trolls. Galador would sound his horn once when all six were inside, and then the dwarves, Rogond and Thorndil would enter from a small passage to the north, which the trolls had blocked. The dwarves had spent the last two days quietly clearing it; it would not take much now to open it wide enough to get through. Then they would bring down the entry and spring the trap.

When Galador winded his horn the second time, the dwarves on the surface would know to remove the stone, letting the light of the full sun into the shaft, magnified and focused by the various mirrors and lenses that had been so carefully placed there. They all hoped the placement was correct—if not, the plan would fail. The light had to be strong and bright; it was unfortunate that they could not test it. Yet the Elves had faith in the abilities of Rogond and Fima, who seemed quite adept at making the necessary calculations. All was in readiness.

When the time came for the Elves to go forth, Gaelen stood before Rogond and embraced him. Then she looked into his earnest grey eyes, and smiled. "All is prepared, Thaylon. This will end well, and we will continue our quest. I have naught but faith in you and your plan. Just be sure those pillars come down."

"I will die a little every moment that you're sealed inside that terrible place, Gaelen. Do not falter, and do *not take this lightly!* If you were taken from me, I don't know what I should do."

"I do not take it lightly, and we will not falter. The plan will work," said Gaelen, who could not imagine that any plan put forth by Rogond could fail.

"That's what you thought of my last plan, the one designed to trap and kill Gorgon Elfhunter, yet he still lives," said Rogond grimly.

Gaelen knew he was troubled by the fact that Gorgon still drew breath. "That was not your failure, beloved. It was mine. It was I who faced him at the end, and I failed to bring him down. I won't fail this time. Those trolls are as good as vanquished. You'll see!" She shook her hair from her bright eyes, her face determined.

Rogond reached up and took her left ear, tracing the elegant, curved tip with a loving hand. "Then let us look to the moment that they fall before you, but be wary of them. They may have powers as yet unknown, for they are of D'hanar. Be ever on your guard, and assume nothing. Keep hard by your bow, Gaelen Taldin. May they fall to your arrows, and to Nelwyn's, should the sunlight fail us." Even as he said this, he felt a deep foreboding. These trolls were *different* somehow.

"We're in luck," said Gaelen breathlessly as she crawled back through the opening into the passage where Beori, Nelwyn, and Galador waited. "Three of them are in the treasury, and the others are feasting down in the ale-cellar. I'm glad they're not all scattered about, as it would make collecting them difficult. This way, I only need lure the three in the cellar up past the treasury, then they will all follow us to the Great Hall and the Chamber of Light. None are there now, so Galador and Beori will have little trouble placing the mirror."

"You are certain that none have detected you? You did not bother to disguise your scent," said Nelwyn.

"They were occupied with their feasting and gloating over their ill-gotten treasure," Gaelen replied. "I did not get close enough to them to arouse them with scent."

"Are you *certain* there are only six?" asked Galador. It was essential to the plan that all their enemies were accounted for.

"Unless they have multiplied, there were only six," said Beori. "Yet I cannot say for certain. We must hope that no others have joined them."

"Indeed," said Nelwyn. "Six will be quite enough for us to handle."

"What are we waiting for?" said Gaelen. "The others are in position, and are awaiting our signal. We dare not miss the high sunlight, and I am quite certain I counted six trolls." She turned then to Galador. "Why must you insist on bringing up such possibilities? Let's get on with the task. I'm going out now, and when next you see me Nelwyn and I will have six trolls pursuing us. You just be ready for them!"

"If I can, I plan to take one or two of them before we get there," said Nelwyn, whose marksmanship rarely failed her. "We may have fewer than six to contend with, if luck is with us."

Galador looked away for a moment. He was annoyed with Gaelen, though he took her meaning. They did not have time to worry about the possibility of more trolls. Yet he wondered...what if there were others that had not been taken into the plan? These might be aroused by the clamor of their fellows, and pose serious threat to Gaelen and Nelwyn, who would not be expecting them. He turned back to his friends, his expression deadly serious, looking Gaelen hard in the eye. "Just be on your guard, that's all."

"We shall, O Mighty Elf of Eádros," Gaelen replied. "And you and Beori take care, as your journey will not be without its hazards. We shall see you in the Chamber of Light." She poked her tousled head through the opening, scenting the air in all directions. Then she slipped easily into the dim chamber where the trolls' torches were barely flickering, and disappeared into the dark.

Nelwyn turned to Galador. "She really does admire you, you know," she said.

"It is of no matter to me one way or the other," said Galador. "Only safeguard yourself, my love, and take no chances without need. We shall either live or die together in this. Farewell for the moment." He embraced her fiercely before releasing her to her task. She vanished into the shadows, as had Gaelen, but only after she turned back to gaze once more upon his anxious face.

The trolls in the cellar had drunk enough ale that they were less wary than usual, and Gaelen had no difficulty slipping in. It appeared that her task would be easier than expected, though she was again impressed with the size of the trolls as they sat amid the ale casks, muttering to one another in their unpleasant voices. A thought struck Gaelen, and she fitted an arrow to her bow, crouching in the dark. Though it was not in their original plan, she would try to shoot one in the eye, as this would probably be her only opportunity. Once they were aware of her, they would be moving too fast. Nelwyn was the better archer, but Gaelen could not pass up the chance, and she took it.

She drew silently on the tiny, glittering eye of the troll nearest her, knowing that she would only kill it if she hit it just right. The arrow would need to go straight in, and to do that, the troll would have to be looking directly at her. She waited, knowing that soon even the most drunken trolls would pick up her scent, and so they did. The one that sat nearest sniffed the air, wrinkling its ugly face in disgust. "Oy!" it said, turning from her for the moment. "What's this I smell? It smells like…like Elf, or I'm a lizard!"

The others grumbled at him. "An' how would you know the smell of Elf, anyway?" they asked.

The first drew itself up importantly. "I've et 'em, thass how!" it said.

The others looked at one another for a moment before breaking into ill-natured laughter, slapping one another hard enough to crack stone. The first looked wounded. "Mind you, they are tasty! I've been wantin' more ever since," it said. "All but the hair. They has this really long hair. I hates long hair…gets stuck, it does."

The trolls' laughter redoubled at this, but in that moment, Gaelen revealed herself. "So, you like Elves, do you? Well, here is one for you, and I don't even have long hair! By the way, you are certainly no lizard, for to call you such would be an affront to lizards!"

Naturally, the surprised trolls all turned their eyes toward her, and when they did so, she took aim and released the arrow. It flew straight to its mark, burying itself in the eye of the one that had boasted of feasting on Elves. The troll gave a screeching howl of pain and reeled back, clutching the arrow in its huge fist. It gave a yank, jerking it free of its now-ruined left eye, black blood streaming from the wound, and howled again.

Gaelen was taken aback. Why had it not fallen? All three trolls roared and leaped to their feet, shaking the ground as they rushed toward her.

"Come here, you Elf-whelp! I'll feast on yer warm liver while yer still alive! C'mere!" yelled the troll Gaelen had wounded. She turned and ran from them, dodging the rocks they hurled at her back, as the plan to reclaim Beori's realm was set into motion.

Gaelen ran as only a Wood-elf being pursued by trolls can run, keeping just out of range of the stones they hurled at her as they followed with huge, heavy strides, shaking the passageway with their thunder. The one she had wounded was in considerable pain, and he led the others, for his motivation to crush the life out of Gaelen was quite high.

Nelwyn heard them coming long before she spotted Gaelen flying toward her. She had positioned herself so that she could take aim at the other three trolls as they came through the doorway from the treasury. They would almost certainly hear the racket and come to investigate. Nelwyn's arrows would distract them long enough for Gaelen to run past; hopefully one or two of the trolls would fall.

Nelwyn crouched in the shadows, caressing the fletching of the arrow she had fitted to the string, her body tense, all her attention focused on the doorway. She was rewarded—two massive, dark shapes appeared with huge, crude hammers in their hands. One stepped into the passage, roaring at the sight of Gaelen. Nelwyn was truly alarmed at the size of it. Gaelen was now near enough for Nelwyn to see the breathless, rather panicked look on her face as she raced headlong.

Knowing that Nelwyn would not fail her, Gaelen set her jaw, breath whistling between clenched teeth, and spurted forward, making straight for the troll that was blocking the passage. The arrow flew just as the troll raised its hammer to strike her, and though it did no lasting damage it provided a successful diversion. A second shaft flew as the troll turned its face toward Nelwyn, roaring. This went straight to its wide open mouth, where it lodged as the troll lashed its head and bellowed in pain and anger. It withdrew the arrow, crushing it in its great fist, as Nelwyn loosed another at the eye of the one that stood behind it.

"Your arrows won't slay them! *Run!*" yelled Gaelen as she flew past, having dodged a hammer-blow from the troll Nelwyn had hit in the mouth. The first three trolls were nearly upon them as well, and all were cursing and bellowing, waving their clubs and hammers.

Nelwyn was fresher than Gaelen, and caught her easily. They raced toward the Great Hall and the Chamber of Light, the stone floor trembling from the trolls' pursuit.

"Why did they not fall to my arrows?" Nelwyn was confused and dismayed.

"I don't know, but I suspect for the same reason that they did not fall to mine," answered Gaelen. "Still, our arrows do pain and distract them. Let's hope they fall to the light, or we're doomed!"

Nelwyn's face was grim as she ran beside her cousin, the angry roar of the trolls filling her ears. Gaelen spoke again, nearly breathless with the effort of keeping her distance. "Did you see all three trolls emerge from the treasury? Are we certain all six are in pursuit?"

Nelwyn thought for a moment. She had, in truth, seen only two enemies in the doorway.

She told Gaelen this, to her dismay. "We dare not pause in our flight to count them. Yet I fear they may not all be accounted for," said Nelwyn. Then they sighted Galador, who stood in plain view in the passage ahead, his longbow drawn, concentrating on the trolls coming up behind Gaelen and Nelwyn.

"Galador! How many foes pursue us?" yelled Gaelen, for Galador would have an excellent view by now.

"I count three, no...four. Yet more can be heard!" he yelled back. "Keep to the passage walls—I am taking aim at the one nearest." He loosed one of his long arrows, and it was a good shot. The arrow hit the troll's mouth, but not directly. It lodged there, to be yanked free at once.

"Don't waste your arrows—these trolls do not fall to them," cried Nelwyn. "Fly, my love!"

All three Elves now fled into the Great Hall, their faces set and determined. A moment later the trolls stormed in after them, halted, and then looked around, blinking dully, grumbling and growling. At last they spotted the Elves, and their huge, ugly faces split into grimaces of rage. "Looks like we'll be feasting on fresh meat tonight," growled one.

"The little one is *mine!*" roared another, who had only one remaining eye.

Gaelen had caught her breath, and now she leaped upon one of the great stone tables, a look of pure dismay on her face. She knew that a subtle deception would be lost on these enemies. She cried out, shrinking back in obviously overstated terror, making sure the trolls would understand her.

"Alas, alas, we shall surely be lost! There are too many of them! We're *doomed!* Oh, dark and dreadful woe!"

She leaped back as the one-eyed troll lurched forward with a bellow, bringing down its great hammer, smashing the stone table with one blow. She turned and fled into the chamber on the heels of Nelwyn and Galador, but as she ran she felt a deep dread growing. These trolls were anything but ordinary, and she had counted only five of them.

There were, indeed, six trolls. It was fortunate that there was not a seventh to worry about. Yet the sixth one, the largest, oldest and most formidable, was too clever to be lured blindly in behind its fellows. Croghi had lived in the realm of D'hanar for a very, very long time. At first a rather ordinary troll, Croghi had changed over the years. He had drunk of the water, and partaken of the air and the soil of that evil land, and thus had grown larger, stronger and more clever than nearly any troll yet living. He had served the Lords Wrothgar and Kotos well, but Croghi yearned for vast wealth...a great hoard such as was heard about in tales. To that end, he had left D'hanar and gone in search of the wealth of dwarves.

Croghi spent nearly all his time in the treasury, gazing raptly at the glittering gold, silver and gems. Belko's wealth was not extensive, but there was much of beauty in it. Trolls do not appreciate beauty, but they do value wealth, even though it is difficult to imagine the use they would have for it. Croghi would kill anyone who attempted to remove even the smallest piece of it.

He was quite capable of doing so, standing just over fifteen feet high, with skin as tough as armor and hands like massive boulders. The other trolls feared him, quite rightly, for he was far cleverer and more corrupt than they. He was the only one among them who wore a helm of iron; it would be nearly impossible for even a well-aimed shaft to find his eyes or his mouth. He had killed Belko, crushing the life from him with one hand before ripping the blood-stone amulet from his neck.

Croghi had been in the treasury with two companions when they first heard the rumbling and bellowing of their fellows, who were pursuing Gaelen. He had lingered there when the others appeared in the doorway to be shot by Nelwyn's bow, and now he followed in pursuit of the Elves, but kept a careful distance. Elves were not entirely new in his experience; he had encountered them before, though not in a long reckoning. Deep in his small mind he knew that Elves could not be taken lightly, and that they were clever. He also knew that the dwarves would try to reclaim their realm sooner or later. The other trolls could not imagine this, for in their minds the dwarves had been defeated so utterly that they would never again be a threat. Croghi knew better.

The hammer he now carried in his right fist weighed about half as much as a horse, and he dragged it as he walked, for he would save his strength. There was something amiss here. No clever Elf would risk such peril when so outnumbered; these must be in league with the dwarves. Croghi would follow at a distance, allowing his brethren to take the brunt of whatever pathetic plan his enemies had devised. Then he would show them the futility of it.

Beori stood upon a large boulder near the entrance to the Chamber of Light, guarding the precious mirror that would mean the difference between victory and defeat. The Elves burst in, followed by their enemies, and Beori prepared for the battle. He would fall rather than retreat, and he was quite ready, his dark eyes glittering, his red beard bristling, clutching a sharp, heavy axe in each hand. Belko would be avenged, no matter what else befell. His folk would not fail him.

Even now, the dwarves were quietly removing the last of the debris blocking their entrance into the Great Hall. Thirty of the stoutest of Beori's folk stood with Thorndil and Rogond. All held large hammers in their hands.

Fima, above in the bright sunlight, listened carefully for the familiar sound of Galador's horn. When he heard it the second time, he would assist in the removal of the stone from the light-shaft. He chuckled to himself as he imagined the startled looks on the faces of the trolls, just before they turned forever to stone.

Rogond crouched just outside the entrance to the Great Hall, listening to the clamor within. The plan had worked reasonably well so far. The trolls had been lured into the hall...that was plain. He heard Gaelen's wailing "cry of doom," knowing it for what it was, and smiled. Yet several minutes had passed, and Galador's horn had not been heard. He was to have blown a blast on it when all six trolls were inside—could it be that not all had been willing to enter?

"We must open the passage, and see what is going on," he told Thorndil and the dwarves. They quietly removed the last of the barrier, and crept into the shadowed hall.

They could hear roaring and smashing sounds from the chamber, but there was still one troll standing outside. Rogond and Thorndil drew back at the sight of Croghi, who was, without question, the largest troll they had ever seen. This troll did not follow the others; it was wary, and apparently capable of thinking for itself. Rogond and Thorndil exchanged looks of dismay. The Elves and Beori would be hard pressed to keep the other trolls at bay, yet Galador would not sound his horn until all six were inside, and this troll showed no such inclination. So long as it stood there, the dwarves would not be able to seal the chamber, and Galador would not give the signal to release the light until the chamber was sealed.

The Elves and Beori faced five angry trolls in the rather confined space of the chamber, and they were hard put to it. They managed to wound the trolls with their bows, yet even Nelwyn's accuracy would not kill them, though she had managed to blind one. Beori swung his axes, distracting them from the Elves when he could, but their hide was so thick that his weapons were notched, and the trolls suffered little from it. One piece of good luck came as Galador drew back his longbow to the limit of his strength, shot one of the trolls in the mouth as it roared above him, and it fell dead. Gaelen and Nelwyn looked at Galador with renewed hope, for it seemed that his bow was more powerful, and his draw was longer. It was just enough to make the difference, and they all took heart. Now at least they only had to contend with one troll each.

Beori ducked under a crushing hammer-blow as he peered outside. There was still one troll remaining in the Great Hall, and it seemed to be debating with itself as to whether to enter the fray. "There is one troll still outside," he yelled breathlessly in the dwarf-tongue, leaping back from yet another hammer-blow. "We must give the signal! Our folk will deal with it. We will never last, and we cannot risk these escaping!"

"No!" yelled Gaelen, who was having her own difficulties evading the troll she had wounded earlier. She answered Beori in the dwarf-tongue: "We must still try to lure it in. Your folk will not be able to bring down the doorway if that troll is there! Give me a moment."

She ran to stand beside Nelwyn, who was fending off the troll she had blinded. It could still smell her, and it swung its hammer back and forth, forcing her to leap out of the way. "Can you hold these two for a minute or so?" asked Gaelen as they both ducked under another crushing blow, shielding their eyes from the sharp chips of stone flying past their faces. Nelwyn nodded, then ran to stand behind one of the large pillars, as Galador took careful aim. His shot went straight into one of the troll's sightless eyes, and it tottered for a moment before falling dead as stone.

Gaelen's mind was working as fast as it could. This troll was the one who liked to sit always in the treasury...she could tell by the golden dwarf-belt he was using as a bracelet. And he was wary for a troll, but not so wary that he could not be deceived, especially if she could somehow appeal to his immeasurable greed. A thought struck her, and she began yelling to Beori in the common-tongue, trying to be heard over the roar of her enemies:

"We must defend this chamber to the last! The trolls have not yet discovered this hidden way! They think they have already taken the treasury, yet this chamber holds the key to the greatest treasure of the Harnian...we cannot risk their discovering it! Hold fast!"

Beori looked confused, then his eyes brightened and he yelled back at her. "Of course! Do not fear... the greatest treasure of my fathers shall never fall. They will never learn the secret of the chamber whilst I live!"

Croghi heard Gaelen's words, and Beori's reply. He was both intrigued and alerted. What were they speaking of? What great hoard was this...surpassing that of the treasury? The greatest in all the Harnian? What sort of vast wealth could be thus hidden? They were speaking now of destroying the way in...he must not allow it! He could not quite bring himself to enter the fray, for he sensed a deception, yet a thing had been awakened in his small mind that he could not ignore.

Gaelen pressed harder, yelling so that the troll would be certain to hear, her words aflame with passion. "Quickly, Beori...we must destroy the hidden way! We must destroy it before they learn of it... we must destroy it *right now!*" She hoped that the troll would soon give in to their ruse, yet he still stood outside, debating with himself. She and Beori tried once more.

"It's no use, worthy Elf...we'll never succeed in keeping the great hoard of my fathers from them. There is no time," yelled Beori. "And if even *one more* enemy should engage us now, all will be lost...we will never be able to hold them off."

"I know," Gaelen called back, "but we must defend the treasure, no matter the cost...why, you compared it with the vast wealth of... ahhh...Fesok the Ironbeard himself! Mountains of Gold! Tons of hard silver! Incredible, bright gems the size of...the size of...my *head!* Yes, the size of my head! And the only thing keeping them safe is this one and *only* way in! And these villains believe that their pathetic hoard encompasses the wealth of the Harnian? *Ha!* If they only knew the truth of it..."

Gaelen could not see whether her deception would work, for a hammer-blow caught her from behind, and hurled her clear across the chamber to strike the wall, falling among the scattered debris of the floor to lie unmoving in the dark.

Beori and Nelwyn cried out in alarm, but Beori kept his wits. "Yes, my friend! Let's destroy it now so that it may never be found again! These trolls must never place their filthy hands upon even the smallest gem..."

Croghi hesitated for only a moment longer. He greatly desired to get to the truth of this "great treasure of the Harnian," and he could not risk Beori destroying the hidden way. If he acted now, he would most likely learn of its whereabouts.

Beori turned to see the last troll rushing into the chamber, his hammer upraised—a more fearsome sight he had never beheld. The troll threw its huge head back and yelled "CRO-GHI!" in a voice like an avalanche.

That thing has a name? thought Beori, even as he knew that this was the troll that had crushed Belko, and he would see it dead. "Give the signal!" he yelled to Galador, who winded his beautiful silver horn, even as he glanced over at the far corner of the chamber where the one-eyed troll was now advancing on Gaelen's motionless form.

Rogond and Thorndil could not hear Gaelen or Beori, but they did see the sixth troll rush into the chamber. They did not wait for the signal, but sped toward the doorway and the great stone pillars. Two lines of fifteen dwarves, followed by Rogond and Thorndil, charged to the doorway and hit one of the pillars with a mighty blow as each passed. The pillars began to totter and crack as Rogond and Thorndil approached; they had been directed to give the final blows that would bring down the doorway.

Rogond roared, swinging with all his might, and then ducked and ran as the stone roof of the passage caved in around him. Thorndil was hit by a great stone, and he fell. Several of the dwarves aided Rogond in dragging him to safety, but no one could breathe for a moment through the choking dust. The Elves and Beori were sealed inside with their enemies. Rogond prayed that the light would not fail them.

The trolls had been distracted by the collapse of the doorway, and the chamber was now in near-total darkness. They recovered quickly, attacking the Elves anew. Croghi was fresh into the battle, and he was a very formidable foe.

Galador and Nelwyn were tiring, but they knew what they had to do. Nelwyn and Beori would have to distract the sixth troll while Galador placed the mirror in the center of the chamber.

Another troll had fallen to one of Galador's arrows; there were now only three to contend with, but this sixth, biggest one was probably worth two of his fellows. The one-eyed troll advanced on Gaelen, though it had learned to be wary of her.

"You may be dead, Elf-whelp, but I'll still feast on your liver, and everything else as well," it said, poking at her with one of its thick fingers. She was wedged in between several boulders, and the troll's large hands would not close on her. It shrugged, imagining the pleasure of dining on her after smashing her into pulp, and raised its great iron-banded hammer.

Outside the mountain, Fima and the dwarves heard the second blast of Galador's horn and sprang into motion, pulling the heavy stone away from the entrance to the shaft. The sunlight was high, though not as high as they had hoped, for it had seemed an interminable time ere they heard the first horn-blast. This second could not come soon enough for Fima—he hoped the light would be bright enough. He and the dwarves of Belko sat together, chanting softly in the tongue of the Rûmhar, willing it to be so.

The mirrors and lenses did exactly as designed, and they were well placed. Galador held the mirror under the now-bright beam of light streaming from the shaft, even as Croghi advanced on him. Nelwyn had sent two arrows into the troll that was threatening Gaelen, but it didn't seem to notice, standing with hammer upraised.

Everyone reeled back from the bright light that now filled every corner of the chamber, for they had been in near-total darkness and it pained them. The trolls were bathed in the bright, golden light of mid-day, and they froze with dread.

Yet the trolls of D'hanar would not be so easily taken. They did not immediately turn to stone as expected, and when they realized that they could still move about they resumed the attack, though the light burned their eyes and pained them. Galador clung with grim tenacity to the precious mirror, focusing the bright beam on each of the trolls in turn, as Croghi rounded on him, unfazed by Nelwyn's arrows or Beori's axe.

Croghi swung one of his great arms at Beori and knocked him hard against the wall, where he lay dazed for a moment. Yet the troll that now turned its attention to finishing him did so slowly and with great difficulty; one could hear its joints grinding and creaking as Beori lay before it. It slowly turned to stone before his eyes, the light finally overcoming it as it struggled to raise its hammer for the last time. The same fate befell the one-eyed troll, but not Croghi, who was moments away from crushing the life from Galador.

Croghi had placed his great foot upon Galador's chest, trying to block the light that streamed from the mirror and crush the life from the Elf at the same time. Galador cried in pain as the troll's huge foot bore down on him. He could not breathe and he felt his ribs bending; in a moment they would break, and he would be crushed.

He groaned and tried to hold the huge weight from his chest with his strong arms, to little avail. Nelwyn and Beori rushed to his aid; Beori hewed the foot with his axe but made little imprint. Nelwyn sent forth arrows at Croghi again and again, trying to divert him. Then, as all seemed lost and Galador's strength faded, the great troll froze as though hesitating, yet his face betrayed his frustration. He could no longer lower his foot to crush his enemy. He tried to roar, but only a wavering growl came out, as his thick, greenish hide turned grey as the stone of the chamber, and was forever stilled.

Beori and Nelwyn knew that Galador's life was ebbing away, for he still could not breathe under the massive weight of Croghi's foot. "Help me! We can save him, but we must act quickly!" Beori cried. Nelwyn was already weeping, but she leaped to Beori's aid, lifting one of the troll's heavy hammers, combining their strength to wield it. They swung hard at Croghi's leg, cracking it at the ankle. One more swing, and the foot came free. Nelwyn had put every bit of strength she had into the effort; she would not be able to raise either of her arms for several days.

Fortunately, Croghi had borne most of his weight on his other leg, otherwise the entire great stone mass of him would have come crashing down. Now Beori shoved the heavy stone foot the rest of the way from Galador's chest as Nelwyn knelt beside him, calling to him, trying to get him breathing again. His face was grey, but there was still some light behind his eyes. He heard her cries and drew a halting, agonizing breath, followed by another, and another.

Beori then heard the crash and clamor of stone as the dwarves broke into the chamber to aid them. They found Nelwyn holding Galador's head in her lap, speaking softly to him as he came to himself. He would breathe painfully for quite some time. She looked back in despair at the corner where the one-eyed troll stood with its hammer forever raised. She did not know whether her cousin was dead or alive.

Rogond finally gained entrance, and he rushed to his friends, looking around the chamber for Gaelen. "She is there," said Nelwyn, who was on the verge of tears, indicating the far corner. "I fear she has taken a deadly blow."

Rogond leaped recklessly over the debris to the corner where Gaelen had lain. "She is not here," he called to Nelwyn. "I see red blood on the stones, but naught else." Then he heard her small voice as she emerged from behind a column.

"We are victorious...everything went exactly as intended...I knew your plan would succeed." She was so badly shaken that she could barely stay on her feet, and her eyes held a faraway look as though fighting to remain aware. Rogond took her and set her down with great care, wiping the blood from her face. She smiled as she looked into his anxious eyes. "We lost no one...even Galador still lives. He is tougher than I thought...I...I shall sleep now." She passed from awareness then, and Rogond lifted her gently and carried her from the chamber.

The dwarves bore Galador with honor, for he had shown tremendous fortitude. The Elves of Eádros and of the Greatwood had redeemed themselves in the eyes of at least some of the dwarves of the Northern Mountains. Fima and the dwarvish healers declared that, with care, both Gaelen and Galador would recover.

The dwarves would celebrate the re-taking of the Great Hall, but the real feast would only be held when their new friends and allies could join them. Soon the stench of the trolls would be cleansed, and the realm truly reclaimed. The trolls would remain forever after, and the tale of how they had been defeated would become one of the favorites told by firelight. The dwarves would shiver as they looked upon the great stone forms, and would be most impressed with the deeds of the three Elves, all of whom had been named "Dwarf-friend".

Chapter 7

The celebration in the Great Hall lasted for days. The dwarves had gone down into their stores to discover many intact ale casks among the ruins, and they had been pleased to find their treasure-stores undiminished. A large delegation from Kino's clan had come 'round on the second day, bringing aid and provisions, for they were good folk at heart. They soon had the place in fine order, for dwarves can display incredible industry when they are motivated. Together with Beori's folk, they put forth such effort that the Hall was bright, cheerful and welcoming in no time, the tables were laden, and every tankard was filled.

Though Kino had sent his people, he did not appear himself. He wondered as to the outcome of the plan—even he had to admit that it was a good one—and he wanted to convey a message to Gaelen, if she still lived. She did, though Rogond and Nelwyn fretted over her for a day or two, as she had gone into a dark slumber from which she did not awaken until the eve of the second night. Until then she had lain with her bright eyes open, muttering over and over about the stars.

Galador recovered well, though it was very difficult and painful for him to breathe. He lay in a quiet corner with Nelwyn beside him. The dwarves were in awe of him when Beori told them the tale. "We were not aware that Elves had such strength," they said. "To have kept from being crushed…and by such a large troll! We cannot imagine it. We bow to you." They dropped their hoods back and bowed in unison before Galador, who found them rather amusing in that moment. He smiled and tried to chuckle, but this proved to be agony for him, and his smile gave way to a grimace of pain.

Rogond came to see him on the morning of the third day, happy to find him sitting beside Nelwyn, taking food and drink. He looked pale, and his pain was evident, but he was improving steadily. He would be right again before long.

Rogond placed a gentle, careful hand on his friend's shoulder. "I know you're still in a lot of pain, yet you look rested. Beori has asked whether you will come to feast tonight, for the dwarves would honor you there. What may I tell him

"You may tell him that I would be most honored to accept his invitation, but only if Gaelen is there as well," said Galador. "She deserves to be honored for her cleverness. Has Beori told you all the tale of the Chamber of Light?"

"He has, and so has Nelwyn. But I don't know whether Gaelen will be with us tonight, for she was still sleeping...I should not disturb her."

Galador looked anxious. "How is she faring? I thought she was surely crushed to death by that blow. Will she be whole again?"

Rogond smiled. He knew that Galador cared very much for Gaelen, though he normally did not show it. "She will be fine, though it would gladden my heart if she would awaken and speak sensibly to me. I would make certain that she is not addle-brained—she took a hard blow to the head, and has spoken no word in awareness since I bore her from the chamber. Yet I sense that I need not worry... she's concentrating on healing herself, that's all."

Galador smiled wryly. "I would not wait too long to hear her speak sensibly, Rogond," he said, his face twisting with pain as he attempted to laugh again. Rogond and Nelwyn shook their heads.

"I'd suggest curtail any jesting at her expense for a while," said Rogond. "Humor is not your friend right now. If I were not such a good friend, I would inform Gaelen of this, then sit back and watch her take advantage of it."

Nelwyn feigned shock, shaking her head. "Why, Rogond! To suggest that Gaelen would take advantage of poor Galador, who of course wouldn't *think* of doing such a thing himself...she would never try to make him laugh if she knew it would pain him. How you misjudge her."

This, of course, amused Galador even more, to his great dismay. "I don't know which is worse," he groaned, "laughing, or trying *not* to!" Nelwyn then grew serious, soothing him and quieting him until he calmed and his pain diminished.

Rogond turned to leave him and return to Gaelen, and as Nelwyn whispered to her life-mate. "My love, do not fear. I have faith in Gaelen. She will be very kind and caring. You'll see."

"Hmmm…I should know soon enough," replied Galador, who did not believe Gaelen capable of resisting such temptation, no matter how kind and caring her cousin thought her to be.

Gaelen came to herself in the late afternoon, to Rogond's great relief. She appeared quite normal in all respects, asking anxiously after her friends, for when she had last seen Galador he had looked none too hale. She wanted to go and see him at once.

No words passed between Gaelen, Galador, and Nelwyn, as none were needed. The three of them embraced silently, eyes closed, each giving thanks for the presence of the others. Rogond smiled to himself. When enough time had passed, and their pain had lessened, Galador and Gaelen would be as testy as ever, but for now it was good to see them express their underlying devotion.

Fima was overjoyed to see Gaelen on her feet. He had been assisting Beori, and had recently settled down to a cask of elderberry wine and the telling of tales. He told the dwarves of the Harnian many stories, for both his supply and his willingness were well-nigh inexhaustible. He was certainly at home here, with a willing audience of eager folk and a full tankard nearly always at his elbow.

When Rogond and the Elves emerged somewhat slowly into the Hall, all fell silent. Fima leaped to his feet, smiling a broad, welcoming smile, and rushed to stand beside them. He made the mistake of clapping Galador on the back, then made for Gaelen as if to embrace her, for he could not contain his enthusiasm. Rogond stepped in front of him. "No, Fima, she is not yet embraceable. You must content yourself with speaking to her for the moment."

Gaelen stepped around him and approached her friend Fima, for she would not deny him. "I would be remiss in not embracing my friend, who came to my aid. I will endure the pain with no complaint." At this Fima put his arms about her as though she were made of spun glass.

Fima directed them to sit at table with him, for Thorndil was already there, looking none the worse for wear. The Company sat united and more-or-less whole, having accomplished their task. Now it would be up to Beori to aid them with news of Hallagond.

First, however, there would be time to make merry. The tales and songs continued far into the night, and the Company was still together as dawn broke above them in the wide world. Nelwyn had spent her efforts in keeping the enthusiastic dwarves from Galador, for they displayed an unfortunate tendency to clap him vigorously on the back. Gaelen, being female, was much less approachable, especially when flanked by Rogond and Fima, who had suggested that anyone who caused her pain would be dealt with personally.

One of Kino's clan drew near to Gaelen and bowed low before her. "I bear a message from Kino for Gaelen Taldin," he said. "He reminds you of your promise to hunt and slay the killer of Noli." Then he bowed again and turned to leave, but Gaelen stayed him.

"Please return this message to Kino from me," she said. "I will keep my promise, I understand his meaning, and I beg his pardon." Then she bowed her head before the messenger, touching her forehead in a gesture of submission. "It is unlikely that I shall ever stand before Kino again, but please inform him that I will send word when the creature that killed Noli lies dead, for I would bring peace to a grieving father."

The messenger nodded. "Your words will cheer him, and he will take them to heart. My thanks, and his, go with you. Good hunting." His dark eyes flashed above the smile he wore. Then he left her.

"You have reassured Kino, and he will remember it," said Fima, patting her arm gently. "Don't be surprised if he actually welcomes you the next time you find yourself in his realm." Even as he said the words, Fima knew how unlikely that would be.

Gaelen shook her head. "I will never go there of my own will again. There is a deep-seated enmity...I can feel it. And it doesn't matter how many times the dwarves of Rûmm say I am welcome, for I know otherwise. I have seen the glances and heard the mutterings."

Fima saw little point in disagreeing with her. He patted her arm again. He understood what she was feeling, for he had occasionally felt it himself while in Mountain-home. *Some Elves and certain dwarves will be forever fettered by conflicts too deep to be completely forgotten.* Fima sighed. It was a pity.

Beori spoke aside to Rogond. "When you are ready, call your Company together, and we will tell everything we know of your brother. But be advised, Aridan, that our knowledge is far from complete, and some of our tale may dismay you. Alas that we cannot take you directly to him, for we do not know where he is at this moment. Perhaps we can set you on the right path, when you are ready."

Rogond nodded. He was ready…he had been ready for some time, yet he took Beori's meaning. It would be best to wait until Gaelen and Galador were strong enough to travel with ease, for once they learned of Hallagond's likely whereabouts they would want to leave straightaway. As welcoming as the dwarves had been to them in recent days, Rogond knew that the Elves would not be content until they roamed freely aboveground, delighting in the scent of the air and the feel of the grass, and most of all the sight of the stars.

Rogond would wait until his friends were strong again, that they might all go forth hale, for there would be trials on the road. He returned to find Gaelen and Fima asleep at the table—Gaelen from simple weariness and the need for healing, Fima from a surfeit of wine. He was snoring as only a dwarf can, so Rogond left him to his dreams. He lifted Gaelen and placed her in a quiet corner, covering her with his cloak to warm her, until she awoke at last to find herself still under his watchful eye.

It was not long before Gaelen and Galador were hale again. Rogond called the Company together, after informing Beori that they were now ready to hear the tale of Hallagond. Beori then sent word to his folk that all who wished to tell of Hallagond should be present, and they gathered in the Great Hall before the roaring fire. Beori looked quite grand as he sat upon his raised dais before them, clad in deep blue and gold. His red beard, intricately plaited, glowed deep auburn like the bright leaves of autumn. There was no doubt that he was the leader of his clan, and he looked it.

With him sat a group of about a dozen stern dwarves, some older than Beori, but many who were still fairly young. They were murmuring to one another in low voices when Rogond, Thorndil, Fima, and the Elves approached and sat cross-legged upon the deep, comfortable cushions that had been set out for them. Food and drink were offered, but few would partake. This would be a solemn council, not a cause for celebration.

Gaelen sat beside Rogond, sensing that what they were about to learn would disquiet him. She spoke so that only he could hear: "Take courage, Thaylon. This is but a stone along our path. We will know the full truth when we get to the end of it…take heart." Rogond nodded, acknowledging her reassurance, though she knew he was still anxious.

Rogond stood before Beori, and told what he had learned from Turanor. Beori and the dwarves nodded gravely; this was consistent with their own knowledge of Hallagond. Then Beori told what he could, and his folk added whatever additional knowledge they would offer. Rogond heard the tales of his elder brother with sorrow, for it appeared that the Rangers' suspicions concerning Hallagond and his disappearance had been correct. His brother was now a man alone...alone and without honor. Rogond knew only that he had last gone to the Eastern Hills, and then possibly to some far-distant land "where no one would know his name."

To Rogond, this was the worst news he could imagine. *I must pick up the trail, and learn whatever I can so that my brother might be found. Perhaps his honor can be restored, though I am in doubt…*

He turned to Gaelen as the tale unfolded, his eyes moist with sorrow and shame. Hallagond had told Beori that he had betrayed his friends and comrades to their deaths. His weakness had doomed them all, and that weakness could never be forgiven. He had forsaken his people, running from any hope of redemption. Rogond sorrowed for his brother, but also for his father and mother, and for all those whose deaths Hallagond had caused. When the dwarves had finished, they tried to console him, but he would not rest now until he had heard the tale from Hallagond's own mouth.

The Company would be leaving upon the next sunrise. As they prepared to depart, Fima came to speak to Rogond. "I know I said I would be going on to Mountain-home, but I have decided to remain with the Company. You will be lost in the Eastern Hills, and I would see this quest through to the end." He paused, gazing past Rogond as though lost in thought.

Rogond looked thankfully down at his friend. "I'm glad you will be going with us, for I fear we shall have need of you. But, are you certain that you wouldn't rather return to the comfort and security of Mountain-home? I'm not certain I would pass up the chance were it open to me."

Fima drew himself up in mock indignation. "Do you think me so old and feeble that I am not up to another journey? I will still be standing when the lot of you are long spent, my friend! I have lingered in Mountain-home too long."

Rogond raised his eyebrows in approval. "Gaelen and Nelwyn will be especially glad to hear that you are coming with us; they could hardly face the prospect of saying goodbye to you. You have won their hearts."

Fima nodded. "I expect I have, as few can resist me should I decide to be at my most charming. Yet the truth is that I cannot bear the thought of saying goodbye to either of them." He looked sidelong at Rogond. "If you tell anyone, I'll have your liver!"

The Company left the dwarf-realm in the early morning, after bidding farewell to Beori and his folk. Thorndil had already returned with their horses. Eros was overjoyed to see Rogond, nearly knocking him over with his large, bony head, while Réalta stood proudly beside Galador as though carved of white marble. Malvorn had been laden with provisions, and Gryffa and Siva stood placidly with their heads down, saving their strength, as they sensed a long journey ahead.

As the Company stood ready to depart, a rather young-looking dwarf approached them with a sturdy stringed instrument known as a Lambalain. The young dwarf's short, sturdy fingers moved over the strings, coaxing forth a wonderful, mellow melody. Everyone drew near and fell silent as the dwarf, bright eyes glittering, began to sing:

"O hearken, ye people, to my golden song,
Of D'hanar's most evil spawn undone.
For three bright Elves with bows swift and strong,
Stood with brave Beori, and our cause was won.

They faced a great enemy, six foes fell and grim,
No others could rival these Children of Stone.
Mighty Belko had fallen, and we would avenge him,
For these foul folk had taken our realm for their own.

Forth stood Taldin, and Thorndil, and Galador the tall,
And Beori, the brave, now the head of our clan,
And golden-haired Nelwyn, the fairest of all,
Would serve to advance clever Aridan's plan.

Through perils unnumbered they strove in the dark,
To lure our foes into that dim council-room,
And when all looked the blackest, and we nearly lost heart,
The bright sun found our foes, and then sealed their doom.

Now our realm is re-taken, and the fires burn bright,
And the Great Hall is bathed in a warm, golden light,
And our tankards are raised, and the stories are told,
Of the fell trolls that fell to our friends brave and bold.

Herein they remain, in their last battle-stance,
For dwarves and tall north-men had made fast the door,
And our people might turn from their hard, stony glance,
But these foes will do harm to our folk nevermore.

Now we bid sad farewell to our proud Dwarf-friends,
And we bless their bright path, and what now lies in store,
And though no one now living can foresee where it ends,
We would hope that it leads to the mountains once more."

Gaelen turned to Fima. "He sings beautifully...better than any dwarf I have yet heard," she whispered. "What is he called?"

Fima did not turn his eyes to her, but spoke under his breath. "You have been favored with a sight hardly ever seen, Gaelen Taldin, for *her* name is Khya. She does, indeed, sing beautifully. Hush, now. Reveal this to no one!"

The dwarf finished playing and bowed low before them, as the Company bowed in return. Gaelen approached Beori, and spoke her farewells in his own tongue. Then she turned and started down the path to the east. Beori looked puzzled, but covered it quickly lest he embarrass her. After she had gone, he shook his head and chuckled, as did several standing near him. It wasn't long after that Rogond's curiosity got the better of him, and he asked Fima about it.

"What did Gaelen say to Beori that so amused him?"

Fima smiled and turned to Rogond, his blue eyes twinkling. "Well, Rûmhul is an admittedly difficult tongue, and many words sound very much alike. I do not believe she really meant to say 'May your beard be forever unruly'." Rogond smiled. He could not wait to inform Galador.

"It seems the mountains want us to be gone," said Gaelen, shaking wet hair from her eyes as she swung aboard Siva. "It was raining when we entered, and it's raining again now. I'm thankful to put my back to the mountains at last."

Galador and Nelwyn agreed. The time under the Northern Mountains had been difficult for all of them. Nelwyn's demeanor was cheerful despite the rain. "I'm so glad to feel the wind upon my face, and smell the green again," she said.

"Still, that wind is chill," said Gaelen, drawing her cloak about her. "Winter will be upon us before we know it. I'm happy to leave the mountains behind, yet the Eastern Hills are far away and will take some time to gain. It will be really cold by the time we reach them." Gaelen was quite used to traveling in cold weather, but the Eastern Hills were said to be a bleak and inhospitable place, largely uninhabited, that could in no way be described as "settled." Only a few dwarves had made their way there, prospecting most likely. She was not comforted.

As the horses made the descent from the gateway to Beori's realm, turning eastward at last, Galador spotted a small figure standing amid the rocks, wearing a grey cloak and a brown hood. The Elves trained their sharp eyes to the figure.

"It's Khya!" said Gaelen.

"Khya? Are you sure?" said Fima, who rode behind her with his arms clasped loosely around her waist. "That would be…most unusual, and not likely."

"I'm quite sure," said Gaelen. Khya raised her right hand, and the Company returned the gesture thinking that she only meant to see them off. "Look," said Gaelen. "She's not bidding farewell… she's beckoning us!" She turned to Fima. "Shall we ride over to meet her, you and I?"

"Good idea," said Fima. "She might be frightened if we all converged on her."

The rest of the Company waited while Fima and Gaelen rode forth to stand below the rain-soaked Khya, who had started to shiver already. Clearly, she was unaccustomed to being outside.

"Hail, Khya of Beori's realm," said Fima. "Do you wish to have words with us?"

Khya nodded, her bright eyes focused on Gaelen. "Indeed, I would speak privately with you, for I have news of Hallagond that Beori does not know. I did not reveal it because Hallagond himself bade me not to." She paused, as though struggling with her own intentions. "I am uncomfortable betraying his confidence, but I would aid you in finding him. He is lost, and in need of you, though he will not admit to it. Your friend Rogond will have a task before him…that is certain!"

Gaelen liked Khya immediately, and her face showed it. "I'm sure Hallagond would understand that you're acting in his best interests. To be honest, we need all the inside information we can get. What news do you bring? We shall be most grateful to hear it."

"Only this," said Khya. "Don't waste your effort seeking news of him in the Eastern Hills, for he has not gone there. He told Beori that this was his plan only to throw off pursuit in the event that someone came seeking him. He went to the vast southland desert, so that he might lose himself. There I expect he remains, if he is yet alive. A more forsaken place I cannot imagine." Khya shuddered at the thought of those distant lands, named Tal-fásath—the barren wasteland—by the Elves.

"How do you know of this?" asked Gaelen. "Hallagond was your friend, wasn't he?" Fima tightened his grip on her arm, as the question was apparently improper. Gaelen, of course, meant nothing by it, and Khya seemed not to take notice, though the end of her small, neat nose reddened just a bit.

"I liked Hallagond, yes, and enjoyed his stories. He was my friend in his way. Why he confided in me I will never know…perhaps he thought it was safe to do so, as I would never be expected to know such things. At any rate, please make sure you put my betrayal of his confidence to good use…it seems I'm not as safe as he thought. Find him…and heal him." She turned to leave, drawing her grey cloak tighter against the wind and rain.

"Sometimes," said Gaelen, "a confidence is best shared with those who care. Farewell, Khya of the Harnian. We are forever indebted to you."

"Just find him. Heal him. He is in need of it," said Khya. "That is all I have to say…farewell, and safe journey." Then she disappeared amid the rocks and the rain.

Gaelen turned back to Fima after Khya had gone. "It took courage for her to come outside the mountain, didn't it? I sensed her discomfort, being alone and unprotected in the open."

"Indeed," said Fima. "Our daughters are kept under very close protection, and they are not inclined to venture into the world. They are rare, and very precious to us. You and I must keep her secret. Now let's go back to the others and share our news."

As Gaelen rode back to rejoin her friends, she kept thinking of Khya. Despite all apparent impropriety, she had been Hallagond's friend. That alone made Gaelen smile. *She has saved us untold time and hardship, and I'd imagine her folk would have been most disapproving of her had they known, yet she did what she knew was right. If I should ever meet her again, I will call her friend—it seems we have much in common.*

The search for Hallagond had begun. Gaelen cast her bright gaze toward the vast sutherlands, away from the Eastern Hills, and urged Siva forward into the next great adventure.

About C.S. Marks

C.S. Marks has often been described as a Renaissance woman. The daughter of academic parents, she holds a Ph.D in Biology and has spent the past three decades teaching Biology and Equine Science. She is currently a Professor Emerita at Saint Mary-of-the-Woods College.

She plays and sings Celtic music; a few examples of her songwriting may be found within the pages of Fire-heart and Ravenshade. She enjoys archery, and makes hand-crafted longbows using primitive tools. A gifted artist, she has produced numerous illustrations for the Alterra books.

Horses are her passion. She is an accomplished horsewoman, having competed in the sport of endurance racing for many years. One of only a handful of Americans to have completed the prestigious Tom Quilty Australian national championship hundred-mile ride, she has described this moment as her finest hour.

She and her husband, Jeff, share their home with an assortment of dogs (predominantly Welsh Corgis) and several wonderful horses. They live deep in the forest, where there are miles and miles of trail riding to be had.

Where to Find C.S. Marks

Website: CSMarks.com

Facebook: Facebook.com/Alterra.CSMarks

Twitter: Twitter.com/CSMarks_Alterra

Goodreads: bit.ly/CSMarks_Goodreads

C.S. Marks Mailing List Sign Up: http://eepurl.com/st8Vj

Book List

Tales of Alterra (The Elfhunter Trilogy)
Elfhunter
Fire-heart
Ravenshade

Alterra Histories
The Fire King
Fallen Embers
The Shadow-man
Iron Promises

Undiscovered Realms
Outcaste

I hope you've enjoyed reading Iron Promises. Please consider leaving a review on Goodreads and your point of purchase.

Made in the USA
Middletown, DE
16 July 2023

35295714R00078